ASH

———

HELL SQUAD #14

ANNA HACKETT

Ash

Published by Anna Hackett

Copyright 2017 by Anna Hackett

Cover by Melody Simmons of eBookindiecovers

Edits by Tanya Saari

ISBN (ebook): 978-1-925539-33-2

ISBN (paperback): 978-1-925539-34-9

Hell Squad – Amazon Bestselling Science Fiction Romance Series and SFR Galaxy Award for best Post-Apocalypse for Readers who don't like Post-Apocalypse

The Anomaly Series – #1 Amazon Action Adventure Romance Bestseller

"Like Indiana Jones meets Star Wars. A treasure hunt with a steamy romance." – SFF Dragon, review of *Among Galactic Ruins*

"Strap in, enjoy the heat of romance and the daring of this group of space travellers!" – Di, Top 500 Amazon Reviewer, review of *At Star's End*

"Action, danger, aliens, romance – yup, it's another great book from Anna Hackett!" – Book Gannet Reviews, review of *Hell Squad: Marcus*

Sign up for my VIP mailing list and get your *free box set* containing three action-packed romances.

Visit here to get started:
www.annahackettbooks.com

CHAPTER ONE

H e planted his boot in the middle of the alien raptor's gut and kicked.

The six-and-a-half-foot dinosaur-like alien fell back with a grunt. Ash Connors lifted his carbine, aimed it straight at the bastard's scaled chest, and fired.

Behind him, Ash heard shouts and then a man's wild laughter. He turned his head and saw the rest of his squad—all wearing dark, scarred armor—taking down the remainder of the raptor patrol. They were standing on an abandoned city street, in the once busy and bustling Sydney, former capital of the now-destroyed United Coalition of Countries.

Big, bearded Hemi Rahia was smiling as he sprayed carbine fire around and finished off another raptor. Beside him, his intense brother Tane, their squad leader, fired his carbine in quick succession, taking down another of the scaled, humanoid aliens.

You fuckers picked the wrong planet to invade. Ash spun, aimed, and fired some more shots.

Nearby, the sunlight glinted off a pair of knives as Dom Santora lunged and slashed at two raptors. His moves were so fast that Ash could barely see the whirl of the blades. On the other side of Dom, Griff Callan relentlessly fought hand-to-hand with another huge raptor. It didn't matter that the alien towered over Griff by several inches. The former cop and ex-con was powerful, and filled with a dogged determination. It also helped that they all wore battle armor that contained slimline exoskeletons, which made them a match for the bigger, stronger aliens.

A husky female voice came through Ash's earpiece. "Three more raptors just popped up to the north of your location. Coming out through a burned-out bank building. Take them down, Squad Three. Make it hurt."

Indy Bennett was their comms officer. She was safely ensconced back at the Enclave, watching drone feed and sending them intel. But not being physically in the fight didn't hide her bloodthirsty streak.

"Ash, watch out!"

Levi King's shout made Ash swing around. He spotted his best friend, the man who was his brother—even though they didn't share blood—sprinting toward him. Like the rest of his squad, Levi didn't wear armor on his arms. As he ran, he pumped his muscled arms, his chest splattered with raptor gore. He swung his carbine up and leaped into the air, kicking out as he went up, and sprayed carbine fire behind Ash.

Ash dropped to his knee, sighting down the scope.

Several raptors burst up from under the pavement, concrete and dirt flying everywhere. Shit, the fuckers had been lying in ambush. One reared up in front of Ash, swinging out with a giant, clawed fist.

Ash ducked, rolled, and came up beside Levi.

His friend grinned. "Ready?"

"Bring it," Ash replied.

Together, they opened fire, the two of them working in unison. They moved forward steadily, keeping up the hail of laser fire. They mowed down the last of the raptors.

When they were done, no raptors were left breathing. Levi let out a laugh and pumped a fist into the air. Ash lifted his carbine up to his shoulder.

"Time to get out of here, Squad Three." Tane's deep voice was a low growl, with a touch of New Zealand in it. His dreadlocks framed his hard face as he pressed a finger to his ear. "Indy, send in a Hawk. We're ready to head back to base."

"You got it, boss-man," Indy answered. "Quadcopter is en route."

"What the fuck is that?" Hemi said.

Ash looked down into the hole where the raptors had been hiding. Inside, giant cables—some as thick as his chest—lay in a tangle. They pulsed and glowed with a red light.

The raptors—proper name for the bastards was the Gizzida—had advanced tech that combined electronics with organics. These cables were scaly, and the way they pulsed reminded him of blood vessels.

"Get some pictures," Tane said.

Griff stepped forward and pulled out a recording device.

"I'll take a closer look," Ash said.

Tane inclined his head. "Do it."

Ash leaped down into the hole. They'd been sent out to this location because the drone team had picked up huge power fluctuations in the area. He looked around. "Looks like an old tunnel. Maybe it was used for maintenance or storm water drainage?"

He touched a gloved hand tentatively to one of the cables. It looked like a giant snake. Damn, they were ugly. What the hell were the aliens doing with them? He took one last look around in the dimly lit passage, then hoisted himself out of the opening and back into the sunlight.

"The Sydney Advanced Distributor Tunnel System isn't far from here," Levi said. "It was dug out about a decade ago, when the traffic problems in the inner city got too bad. There's an entire system of traffic tunnels under the city center."

Ash's gut tightened. "And now the Gizzida are using it. Protected and out of sight. Damn."

A muscle ticked in Tane's jaw. "Get the pics. We'll take the intel back to the general, and see what he wants to do about it."

As Griff took more images, Ash walked over to an overgrown strip of grass near the crumbling sidewalk and scrubbed his boot against it to clean off some of the gore.

"Fuck me." Beside him, Levi grinned and stretched his arms over his head. "I'm pumped after that fight. I need a woman. I could fuck all night long."

Ash shook his head and smiled. Levi fought hard,

played hard, and lived hard. He always had, even when they were boys. Levi had taken over the Iron Kings Motorcycle Club in Sydney at the age of twenty-one, in a messy coup. He'd been young, but he'd fought, bled for it, and sacrificed everything to pull the club out of the darkness their old leader had sunk it into.

Levi had always been brilliant with bikes, cars, and engines. He could make anything purr—from a modified motorcycle, to a custom car, to a woman. And Ash had been by his side through almost all of it. Since the aliens had invaded, the world had turned into a fucked-up place, and the Iron Kings were long gone. Ash paused for a second to think of his lost brothers. Through everything, there was one thing Ash had never doubted, and that was Levi's loyalty. His best friend was loyal to the bone.

"You need a pretty, energetic thing, too, bro." Levi swung his carbine up onto his shoulder. "Take the edge off."

"You worrying about my love life, King? You want to paint my nails, too?"

Levi snorted and together they walked over toward the others. "Where you stick your dick is up to you. But you have been spending a lot of nights alone."

Ash cast a look at his friend and saw a glint of worry on Levi's face. "I'm fine, Levi."

His friend studied him hard. "If you're not, you let me know."

Ash lifted his closed fist and they bumped knuckles. They'd first bumped knuckles as six-year-olds, after they'd beaten the hell out of each other behind the Iron

Kings clubhouse. Ash couldn't remember, but he was pretty sure their fathers had been inside drinking or fucking. In the battle to prove who was the bigger six-year-old badass, it had turned out to be a draw, and a lifelong friendship had been forged.

And now, for two years, they'd been fighting the invading aliens. The Earth had been devastated, leaving pockets of humanity to run, hide, and fight for survival. He and Levi had joined the Squad Three berserkers and were part of the frontline, pushing back against the aliens. This was a dark, dirty job, and some days it was a heavy weight.

"Hawk's here," Tane called out.

Looking up, Ash caught a glimmer in the blue sky above. The quadcopter was coming in with its illusion system up. As it neared the ground, it dropped its illusion, and he studied the dull, gray hull and the four spinning rotors. The aircraft ran on a small thermonuclear engine, with the rotors shrouded, so it was silent, giving no sign of its presence—with the exception of the dust it kicked up around them.

It hovered a couple of feet above the ground, and Tane leaped up on the skid and pulled the door open. They all jumped inside.

"Welcome aboard," the pilot, Finn Erickson called back from the cockpit. "Clear skies are forecast, but buckle up in case of any alien-induced turbulence."

"Just fly the Hawk, Erickson," Hemi hollered.

Levi settled back in a seat. "When we get back to the Enclave, how about we grab some dinner, a few beers, and then we find some feminine company?"

"Beer sounds good," Ash said. "After that, I have—"

"—plans." Levi's gaze narrowed. "Is it a woman? You holding out on me, Connors?"

Ash leaned back. "You sure you don't want to paint my nails?"

From behind them, Hemi chuckled.

"Fuck you," Levi said good-naturedly, dropping his head against the headrest.

Tane slammed the door closed, and a second later, the Hawk shot upward into the air. Ash stretched his legs out in front of him, and crossed them at the ankles. He turned his head to look outside, catching one last glimpse of the strange cables buried in the ground. He was sure the geek squad would be able to work out what the hell the aliens were doing, and how to stop them.

The geek squad. Instantly, his thoughts turned to a pretty, curly-haired member of the tech team who watched him with a wary gaze. Marin Mitchell, who looked cute as hell, had a husky voice designed to drive a man to think dirty thoughts, and a brilliant mind. He exhaled slowly, picturing her sweet curves.

The Hawk banked at that moment, and Ash's attention turned back to the window. The ground below was nothing but devastation, stretching out as far as he could see. His hands curled into fists. He had grown used to seeing it. The abandoned houses, toppled skyscrapers, burned-out shops, overturned vehicles, and overgrown yards and parks. All destroyed. He knew it was the same all over the planet. Every now and then, though, it hit him hard that the world as they knew it was gone.

He released a frustrated breath. He knew better than

anyone that anything good never stayed around. Once, he'd tried to take what he wanted, grab onto his passion and build a better life for himself. He tasted the sweet and the fresh, but then life had slapped him down. Life always turned around and slapped everybody down.

He leaned his head back against the seat and closed his eyes. If there was one thing he'd learned in life, it was not to reach for things he didn't deserve.

———

"DINNER. NOW."

Marin Mitchell huffed out a breath and lifted her gaze to look at her boss. She had her glasses on, so it took a second of blinking before her vision adjusted, and his hawkish face came into view. Noah Kim had a handsome face, and straight, black hair and dark eyes, thanks to his South Korean heritage. As usual, he was scowling.

"I've got work to finish," she said.

Noah crossed his arms over his chest. "You haven't stopped all day. I don't need you fainting in my tech lab."

Marin eyed the stacks of alien data cubes piled on her desk. She'd gotten data off a bunch of them, but some had extra layers of encryption, and she was determined to break them. They'd been brought in a few weeks ago by one of the berserkers. The image of the handsome, sexy man with gorgeous, colorful tattoos that traveled up and down his arms drifted through her head. Then she squelched it. She wasn't supposed to be sitting here daydreaming about badass men who were so far out of her league it wasn't funny.

She picked up one of the cubes. "I'm close to breaking the encryption on these last cubes. I got through one, and the info on here talks about an alien data hub. Some central hub where the aliens are storing their information. *All* their information, Noah."

Noah's gaze was unwavering. "That's great. Dinner. Now."

With a huff, Marin set the cube down. "You know you're bossy, right?"

"Yep."

She followed him out of the tech lab, passing around benches loaded with bits of electronic wiring and computer guts.

"I don't know how Laura puts up with you."

Noah shot Marin a look, and then smiled. It relaxed his entire face, and made him even more handsome. "I make up for my bossiness in other ways."

Marin held up a hand. "Please, don't say anything else. I don't want to know." She didn't need the mental images of the couple in her head underscoring her own lack of any sort of romantic relationship.

They headed out into the hall. Laura was Captain Laura Bladon, head of the interrogation team and prison cells. To say that the arrogant Noah and the serious Laura had struck sparks off each other initially was...an understatement. But now, the fiery couple was one hundred percent, passionately in love.

Marin had never been in love.

A sigh escaped her. All her life, she'd dreamed of having someone who loved her for her. Someone who looked at her and got that same hot spark in his gaze she saw in Noah's when he looked at Laura.

But Marin had been the typical too-smart, too-geeky, too-absorbed-with-other-things student at school. She didn't know the first thing about wearing trendy clothes, or putting on makeup. As her jeans and baggy, blue-checked shirt attested, she liked to be comfy.

It hardly mattered what she wore. The good-looking guys at school had never given her a single glance. At university, some of them had wised up a little and she'd dated a bit. But no one had ever really set off any sparks.

She pushed her glasses up, and headed into the dining room after Noah. It was then she realized that her shirt had an ink stain on the front of it, and her untamable hair was in a messy nest of curls that she'd tied up on top of her head. She was pretty sure she'd lost a pen in there, somewhere, too.

Oh, well. Not much she could do about it, and besides, she wasn't trying to impress anyone.

In the dining room, many of the Enclave's residents were already seated at tables, laughing, chatting, and eating. She followed Noah over to where some of the other tech team guys were already hunched over plates of food.

"Sit. I'll get you a plate." When he stalked off, she barely resisted poking her tongue out at his broad back.

The guys at the table called out hellos. They were an amazing team to work with. The Enclave had some of the world's best tech minds, and once they added Noah and the remnants of the team from Blue Mountain Base, Marin had to admit they were pretty darn formidable.

She sat down beside Eric, a lanky guy with sandy hair in need of a cut, and glasses. "Hey, Marin. How are the cubes coming along?"

She nodded. "Getting there."

"You playing in the Pre-Emptive Strike battle tonight?" Eric's blue eyes lit up. "Everyone's going to be playing, and looking to take you down."

She smiled. This was the other reason she'd been pushing so hard to get her work finished. The computer game was one of the highlights of her life. "I'll be there. And I'm gonna kick your ass."

Some of the others responded to her comment with wisecracks and good-natured grins. Eric smiled. He really was cute in a sweet, geeky way. If only she'd felt a spark of attraction to him...

"You want to team up?" he asked hopefully.

Her heart knocked against her ribs, and she gave him a small, apologetic smile. "I already have a fight partner." Excitement sizzled through her. She couldn't wait to sign on tonight and join up with him again. Since they'd connected in the game a few weeks ago, they'd played together almost every night, and become an unstoppable duo.

Eric's face fell. "Right. The mysterious Super-Soldier3."

"Yes." Marin scanned the table, and then the dining room. She had no idea which gamer geek was her mystery fight partner. She swallowed. She just prayed he wasn't some teenage boy pretending to be older.

A part of her screamed at her to ask SuperSoldier who he was, but another part was too afraid. They played well together, and then stayed online on the base's network afterward, talking. Sometimes for hours.

She knew his childhood hadn't been great. His mom had left, and he and his sister had been raised by his dad. Who, to Marin, didn't sound like he'd win father of the year. SuperSoldier had confessed he'd gone to college, been so excited to start a new life, but his sister had gotten mixed up with drugs, and so he'd dropped out to help his dad. He'd ended up working in the family business.

Marin had told him about growing up with a never satisfied mother and an oblivious father. She'd told him about feeling more than a little awkward in social situations. She knew she wasn't terrible to look at, but parties or social gatherings made her uncomfortable, and it was hard work to keep a smile on her face. She'd told him about loving her work, and her driving need to learn and figure out problems.

She really liked him.

Every time she was online, she thought about asking his real name. But, truth be told, she was too afraid she'd be disappointed, or worse, *he'd* be disappointed if they revealed their true identities. She didn't want to ruin the fantasy.

A commotion at the doorway made her look up. A group was entering the dining room. *Hell Squad*. Her breath hitched as she watched them. Marcus Steele strode in, his arm around his wife, Elle. They made such a fascinating couple. The battle-hardened soldier, and the smart, sweet comms officer. The big, tough man was completely in love with Elle. They gave Marin hope that one day, even in the chaos the world was now, she'd find something like what they had. Although Elle was also a former socialite. She was the kind of woman that Marin's mother would have loved to have as a daughter. Helena Mitchell had been constantly perplexed by her daughter.

The woman who followed Marcus and Elle made Marin sit up straighter. Claudia Frost was the only female soldier in Hell Squad. The woman was tall, tough, and badass. She was wearing khaki cargos and a dark T-shirt, walked with a slight swagger, and exuded confidence. She was Marin's hero. Oh, who the hell was she kidding? She was Marin's girl crush. Claudia was everything Marin wanted to be in her dreams.

A man followed one step behind Claudia. With shaggy brown hair that contained gold strands, and an easy smile, Shaw Baird was pretty easy on the eyes. He slung an arm around Claudia's shoulder and the woman elbowed him in the gut in response. But a second later, he pulled her in for a quick kiss, and Claudia clearly didn't mind.

The rest of Hell Squad and their partners followed behind. These were the men and women who went out there every day to fight the Gizzida. Every day, they risked their lives to keep the Enclave safe. They were heroes.

Marin knew she was doing her part with the tech team. They kept the power on, the water hot, and the systems running, and they helped decode alien tech and information for the squads.

But she knew it wasn't nearly the same thing as putting on armor, picking up a carbine, and climbing into a Hawk to face the aliens.

She toyed with the food on her plate, only half-listening to the flow of conversation around her. She always felt like this...always on the edge, trying to do her best, but never feeling like it was enough. Like she was enough.

God, Marin. You're in the middle of an alien apocalypse. Suck it up.

Suddenly, she heard the sound of deep voices and raucous laughter filled the room.

Another group entered the dining room, and the air caught in her lungs. The berserkers had arrived.

She watched, riveted, as the all-male squad passed through the doorway. The berserkers were rough, tough, and dangerous. From what she'd heard, they didn't all have military training. In fact, a few of them had rather dubious backgrounds. Former mercenaries, bikers, criminals...

They were the most amazing men she'd ever seen, and she could admit that something about them made her insides quiver. They were all big, muscled, and covered in tattoos. She glanced around the room and noted more than a few women staring.

The head of the squad, Tane, had brown dreadlocks that fell around his dark, intense face. His brother Hemi was shorter, and a little broader. He had a dark beard and a booming laugh. Both men's arms were covered in amazing Maori-style tattoos.

Griff was talking with Dom. The former cop had hair clipped short and a powerful body. She knew Griff had gone down for some crime, and she wondered again just how a cop survived in prison. In comparison, Dom was all darkness. He moved in a fluid, elegant way that made you want to just watch him walk. He had a lean face, black hair and black eyes. Something about him always set off Marin's hindbrain, telling her to hide or run.

Levi had his gold-streaked brown hair pulled up in a man-bun at the back of his head. If any of the tech team tried that hairstyle, she knew they'd look silly. Levi, however, did not.

Then her gaze fell on Ash Connors.

Her pulse spiked. He was a little more handsome than the others, but no less sexy or dangerous. Both his arms were covered in sleeves of ink in shades of black, red and blue. She loved looking at those tattoos. Every time she did, she saw different images in them.

As she watched, two women sauntered up to the berserkers, all smiles and flirty looks. Levi grinned at a curvy brunette and tugged her in close. The other woman, who was tall with a fall of honey-blonde hair, leaned into Ash.

Marin looked down at her plate. Those were the kind of women big, wild, sexy men liked—gorgeous, confident, and sexy. All the things she wasn't. She glanced at her watch. There was still a bit of time until the Pre-Emptive Strike battle, but she suddenly wasn't hungry anymore.

"I'm off." She grabbed her dishes, stood, and nodded at the rest of her team. "See you on the battlefield."

After she cleared away her dinnerware, Marin headed back to her room. She liked the Enclave. It had been purposely built in an underground coal mine to serve as a sanctuary by the Coalition's former, and very corrupt, president. There was a lovely garden, a hell of a computer system, and even artwork on the walls to brighten the place.

After pressing a hand to her door lock, Marin stepped into her quarters and flicked on the lights. She knew it was the same as others in the base had—small living room with a kitchenette, and a bedroom off to the side with a tiny bathroom. It wasn't much, but it was home, and she was grateful for it.

She'd loaded her bookcase with books she'd snagged from wherever she could find them, and had a kickass computer and screen set up at the desk pushed against the wall. She eyed the widescreen. She'd scavenged the parts for the comp herself, and knew she had one of the sweetest gaming setups in the Enclave.

Marin took her time changing into some comfy, cutoff jean shorts, and a clean T-shirt. Then she cleaned up the clothes she'd dumped on the floor over the last few days. She wasn't the messiest person in the world, but when she got busy with her work, she sometimes let the housework slide. She wrinkled her nose. Housework was so overrated.

Finally, she glanced at her watch. She stroked the face of the men's watch. It had been her father's. It was all she had left of her absentminded, smart, but loving dad.

Her pulse jumped. The game was starting. She sat down at her computer and pulled on her headset.

Time to kick some ass.

CHAPTER TWO

Marin logged into Pre-Emptive Strike, atmospheric graphics filling her screen. She knew some of the tech team had virtual reality goggles to play with, but not that many sets had survived the attack.

She tapped the screen and activated voice control. Her character appeared. PrincessBadass lived up to her name. Tall, muscular, with straight, blonde hair that was pulled back in a ponytail. Marin's character carried a carbine that glowed pink. Every time Marin saw her avatar, she smiled.

She checked the login screen. Her partner was late. She felt a little flutter and bit down on her lip. Maybe he wouldn't show up tonight?

At that moment, a dialogue box popped up on the screen, and words started to appear. *How's my badass princess tonight?*

Marin smiled. A huge, tough soldier appeared on the screen, towering over her character. He had cool, battle-scarred armor, dark hair cut super-short, and black ink down one arm. SuperSoldier3.

"Hey, you," she said into her headset. She knew that somewhere in the Enclave, he'd be watching the words appear on his screen.

Ready to kick some ass?

Marin flexed her fingers. "Always."

Others began to join the game, and a timer appeared, counting down to the start of the fight. Tonight, they'd be battling giant mutated animals that had broken out of the Earth's crust to destroy the world.

Did you have a good day?

She thought of the alien cubes. "Yes, and pretty productive. You?"

Uneventful.

Three, two, one. The battle began.

Let's move along that brick building. Watch out for anything falling off the roof.

She moved in sync with SuperSoldier3. He was always very strategic, thinking of cover and vantage points. They hugged the wall, turned a corner, and faced an incoming mob of monsters.

Marin's fingers danced over the controls. Princess-Badass lifted her carbine, and fired. Together, they plowed into the mêlée. When her ammo ran dry, Super-Soldier3 was there, tossing her more. When a monster burrowed right up beneath him, Marin leaped in close and shoved a healing pack his way.

They fought side by side, watching each other's back. Marin mowed down three wild beasts.

Nice work. His character spun and jammed a wicked blade into the gut of an oncoming monster.

"Not too shabby, yourself," she said.

As she watched other players' characters going down in the onslaught, she imagined that this was just the tiniest taste of what it actually felt like for the squads to be out there, battling the Gizzida in real life. She shivered. Even just playing the game got her heart pumping and anxiety tensing her muscles. She felt fear, stress, elation, and frustration.

How would it feel to know it was real? To know one wrong move could mean your death?

She knew she'd never be brave enough or strong enough for that.

Incoming. Twelve o'clock. SuperSoldier3 moved in close to her.

Marin saw a giant, multi-legged monster pull itself out of a hole in the ground. Then she spotted movement behind them. "We have a pack of crushers coming in from the rear."

The crushers looked like dog-like apes, moving with a loping gait on their large front legs.

She pressed her back to SuperSoldier3's and started firing her weapon. She grabbed several grenades off her belt and tossed them. The roar of SuperSoldier3's carbine echoed around her.

They fought, and then ducked for cover. Tucked behind a wall, Marin popped up to fire, her shoulder pressed to SuperSoldier3's hard one.

They're getting too close.

"Cover me." Marin touched the controls. Princess-

Badass leaped over the wall, pulled out a huge grenade, and ran straight at the group of monsters. He laid down cover fire, and she tossed the device. Rolling out of the way, she jumped up and sprinted back toward Super-Soldier3.

The controls shook in her hands as the grenade exploded. Her character dived over the wall and landed beside him. The screen exploded with flames and rearing, screaming monsters.

That was badass.

Warmth burst in her chest. She'd never truly been badass before. The last monster tottered sideways, then collapsed.

Suddenly, words appeared on the screen. *Battle winners. PrincessBadass and SuperSoldier3.*

Blood pumped thickly through Marin's veins. She flexed her stiff fingers, and grinned. Congratulatory messages from other players popped up on the screen. She threw her arms into the air. "We are the champions of the Enclave!"

Loved that move at the end.

"Thanks. I wish I was that fierce in real life." She dropped back in her chair, staring at his words on the screen.

And, right at that moment, she wished she knew who he was.

I bet you're fiercer than you think. I love watching you kick ass. It's sexy as hell.

Marin felt heat in her cheeks. "My character is sexy. I designed her like that." The opposite to real-life Marin.

She knew she was smart, and not unattractive, but sexy escaped her.

Sexy has nothing to do with what you look like, Princess.

She stilled, her gaze riveted to the blinking cursor.

And it has nothing to do with your character in the game.

Her breath hitched. She knew what was coming.

The words came up on the screen. *You want to have some fun again? Celebrate our win?*

She watched the blinking cursor, heat curling through her belly. "Yes," she whispered.

Good. Unbutton your trousers, Princess.

Marin couldn't exactly remember how this had started. A week into their gaming partnership, they'd started talking. Sometimes for hours in the middle of the night. She'd told him things she'd never told a soul before.

And then one night, things had turned...hot. Sexy.

Did you open them?

Marin leaned back in her chair and flicked open the button on her shorts. "Yes." Her voice was breathy.

Good. Now, press your hand to your belly.

In her head, she imagined his voice—deep, low, and sexy. She could almost feel the brush of his warm breath on her neck. She did as he commanded, sliding her hand down her quivering belly.

Go lower, Princess. Slide two fingers inside your panties.

God. She closed her eyes, her fingers sliding under silky cotton. She imagined a big, masculine hand moving over her belly and between her legs. In her fantasy, that arm was covered in tattoos. Strangely, they weren't the black designs on SuperSoldier3's character, but splashes of ink in different colors.

Are you wet?

"Yes." Her panties were soaked. Her belly was tight, desire pooling inside her.

Touch yourself, Princess.

She stroked herself, a gasp escaping her throat. That felt so good.

I bet you're so damn pink and pretty. How wet, Princess?

"Wet." She knew if he was here in the room, she'd never have the courage to talk to him like this.

Touch your clit.

Marin did, pressing that swollen nub in small circles. Sensations flared outward inside her, and she cried out.

Fuck. I wish I could hear you. See you. Touch you.

Open-mouthed, she stared at the words on the screen. "Are you...touching yourself?"

Hell, yeah. My cock is in my hand and it's so fucking hard.

Marin moaned and sank her teeth into her lip. She could imagine it.

Now, slide a finger inside yourself.

For the last two years, Marin had only had self-induced orgasms. She usually only gave her clit attention to get the job done and relieve a little stress. "I haven't done that much lately."

Baby, you're killing me.

She wondered if he was groaning. Wondered what he was feeling. She slid her finger inside herself, gasping.

How's it feel?

"Good." But not enough. She needed more to fill the emptiness.

Tell me how you taste, Princess.

Taste? She blinked. "What?"

Lick your fingers, baby.

Was she brave enough? She trembled, feeling her orgasm looming.

Be fierce, Princess.

Seduced and feeling so hungry, Marin lifted her fingers to her lips and tentatively licked. She tasted musky, different, not unpleasant. "It's different."

I bet it's the tastiest honey. Now, rub your clit some more.

Her hand moved back into her shorts, and she found her rhythm, her hips jerking.

You're going to come for me now.

"Yes." Her head slammed back against her chair, and she kept working her clit. She imagined a big, tough body kneeling between her legs, a dark head between her thighs.

"SuperSoldier..."

Right here. Come for me, Princess.

Her muscles tensed and sensation exploded through her. She cried out, throwing herself back against her chair. *So. Good.*

As the orgasm subsided, and the world around her came back into focus, she blinked. She was sprawled in her chair, a boneless mess.

Did you come, baby?

"Yes. Hard."

I'm in agony here. You are so sexy. Never forget it.

"I'll try," she whispered.

Good night, Princess.

"Night, SuperSoldier."

She watched as the text disappeared from the screen. He'd logged off.

Marin looked up at the ceiling and worried her bottom lip. She had the skills to hack the system and see where he was in the Enclave. It would be easy to work out his identity.

But if he wanted to change their relationship, he'd ask her, right? She huffed out a breath. She wished she was brave enough to tell him that she wanted to meet him.

She sat there for a long moment, belly tight, not quite able to find the courage.

Then her computer made a soft *ding*. Excited, she scrambled up. Maybe he was contacting her to suggest they meet?

Marin scanned the screen and her shoulders drooped. It was a message from Noah. She quickly did up her shorts. He'd scheduled an early meeting first thing in the morning. One of the squads had seen something on a mission, and they needed Marin to take a look at the images.

With a sigh, Marin stood. Time to get ready for bed. Alone.

ASH STROKED his cock with hard, firm pulls. A groan ripped out of him. In his head, he thought of sexy, smart

Marin Mitchell sprawled out before him, with her skin flushed and her thighs wet.

Pressure coiled around the base of his spine. He grabbed the T-shirt he'd discarded earlier off the bed. His orgasm hit him with the strength of a grenade blast. With a groan, he spilled in the fabric bunched in his fist.

Fuck. He dropped back into his chair, and stared at his comp screen. Somewhere in the Enclave, he knew his gaming partner was still getting her breath back, her muscles relaxed and the soft folds between her legs swollen and sticky.

Ash groaned again. The pretty tech team member had no idea he was SuperSoldier3. If she did...well, Ash wasn't sure what she'd do. He wasn't sure when his little fascination with Marin had started. He'd caught glimpses of her here and there back at Blue Mountain Base, and the first time he'd heard that sexy voice of hers—huskier and deeper than he'd expected—it had given him ideas. But it had all been cemented a few weeks ago, when he'd dropped off some alien cubes in the tech lab, and noticed she played the game he sometimes enjoyed.

He'd played around on Pre-Emptive Strike when he'd first arrived at the Enclave, but since he'd started playing with Marin, those hours had become some of the best for him.

Damn. A part of him wanted to storm through the Enclave corridors and find her. Push her back on her bed and put his hands on her. He wanted to touch her between her legs and hear her breathy cries as she came. He wanted to claim her and make sure she knew who she belonged to.

He blew out a long breath and stood. He tossed his shirt in his hamper, stripped off his jeans, and strode naked into his bathroom. He flicked on the shower.

As steam filled the stall, he stared at his reflection in the mirror. He saw the tattoos, and a few scars, too. Each rough mark on his skin was a testament to the life he'd led. He knew exactly what he was. A fighter, a biker, a big man with tough hands who got the job done.

Once, he'd had a shot at a different life. University had been fucking amazing. Growing up in the motorcycle club had been pretty rough. But then, going to college, playing ball, studying to be a doctor...it had been a bright, shiny world he'd never known had existed. He'd dreamed of helping people, of putting people and things back together, not breaking things. He'd had pretty, cute sorority girls throwing themselves at him, he'd been acing his classes. The future had been wide open.

Until it had all been jerked away.

Ash shrugged off the old, hard feelings. He lifted a hand and flexed it, studying the scars that ran across his knuckles. Some had come from fights as a kid, some from being Levi's right-hand man in the Iron Kings. More still from battling the raptors.

Whatever the reason he had them, he knew that Marin deserved more than what he could offer. It would be a disgrace to put his rough, scarred hands on her smooth skin. Hell, who was he kidding? She'd run long before he even got close.

After a quick shower, he slung a towel around his hips and stared into the mirror, again. Maybe it was time to quit gaming and torturing himself by letting himself have this tiny taste of Marin.

The comms unit beside his bed chimed. He saw he had a message and quickly listened to it. It was from Indy. Looked like they had a meeting in the Command Center in the morning.

After that, there would be another mission. There was always another mission, always more aliens to fight.

The Gizzida invasion had changed everything. The Iron Kings, the men he'd called brothers, were gone. But thankfully, he still had Levi, and now he had new brothers in his squad. The berserkers were the baddest motherfuckers he'd ever fought beside.

Ash dropped onto his bed, staring at the ceiling. He was good at fighting. He needed to stick to what he knew. And that didn't include pretty, sexy tech geniuses.

But something told him that despite his best efforts, his dreams were going to be full of a cute face and a mass of blonde curls.

CHAPTER THREE

The next morning, Marin walked into the Command Center a few minutes before the meeting. The glass doors whispered open, and her gaze snagged on all the screens. She loved the energy of the Command Center...there were always too many people, and a sense of carefully controlled chaos.

People were tapping at comps, leaning over comp screens, huddled in small groups deep in conversation, or moving back and forth through the room. This was the hub of all the operations at the Enclave. If a squad was out in the field, the mission was monitored from here. Straight ahead, she spotted Noah standing near a comp, with a petite brunette seated in front of it. Elle Steele.

"Good morning," Marin called out, as she approached.

Noah raised his eyes, his dark gaze zeroing in on her. "You look...relaxed."

Damn, did her panty-melting orgasm from the night before show? "I slept well."

Her boss tilted his head, his expression curious. "Are you seeing someone?"

"What? No." Her voice came out a little high-pitched, and her cheeks tingled in embarrassment. Clearing her throat, Marin focused on the comp screen. "Hi, Elle."

Hell Squad's comms officer smiled. "Hi, Marin."

"You're looking over the data I decoded off the cubes?"

The woman nodded. "There's some great stuff here."

"I'm glad it can help." Elle was the closest thing they had to an expert in the raptor language.

"There are a few places I'm still not sure about." Elle scrolled, and pulled up some of the slash-like raptor text.

As Elle asked questions, Marin leaned over, closer to the screen, excitement trickling through her. She loved the challenge of decoding a problem, of untangling strands, and working things out. She loved testing herself.

"I still have a few more cubes that I'm working to break the encryption on," Marin said. "But do you see this?" She pointed. "And this? There are several references to a central data hub."

Elle sat back, frowning, and Marin bit back a small sigh. Even with her brow furrowed and her lips pursed, Elle was so pretty. Her hair was neat and shiny, and her figure so slim and elegant. Marin pushed a stray curl back behind her ear, then tugged self-consciously on the hem of her shirt. Her mother had dreamed of Marin being similar to someone like Elle. Pretty, polished, and poised.

Marin let out a breath. Her mother was gone. Both of her parents were. She'd already grieved for her loving but workaholic father, and her complicated mother. There was no need to reopen old wounds.

The world had gone to hell, and Marin knew she was smart and skilled. She helped, in her own way, to fight back against the aliens. She imagined taking her imaginary pink carbine to her past insecurities.

"You're right."

Elle's voice broke through Marin's daydream.

Elle smiled. "There are some very clear references about a data hub. This is really important." Excitement underscored the woman's voice.

Marin nodded, Elle's energy contagious. "Imagine, a central repository of all Gizzida information."

"So where is it?" Noah asked.

Marin's shoulders sagged and she shook her head, the curl she'd tucked away falling forward again. "That's the only thing I haven't figured out, yet. So far, the location hasn't been listed on any of the cubes."

"Maybe it's in the cubes you haven't decrypted yet?" he suggested.

Just then, the doors behind them opened, and two men strode in. Marin straightened. They might be very different in appearance, but they both caught a woman's gaze and kept it.

General Adam Holmes and Niko Ivanov were the co-leaders of the Enclave. The general had created Blue Mountain Base, and saved so many lives in the process. He was tall, with an aristocratic face, and hair going gray at the temples. He exuded authority.

When Blue Mountain Base had been attacked and destroyed by the aliens, General Holmes had been the man to lead them safely to the Enclave. Niko was the civilian leader here. He was an artist, with dark, sexy looks, and an air about him that hinted he knew his way around more than a paintbrush. Marin recognized dangerous when she saw it.

Noah stepped forward. "Let me tell you what Marin found."

The men listened intently, their faces sharpening.

"We need to find this hub," Holmes said.

"That's why I've arranged for Squad Three to join us this morning," Noah said. "They saw something on their mission yesterday that could give us more information, and maybe even lead to the hub."

Squad Three was coming? Marin pressed her suddenly sweaty palms together. The doors whooshed open again.

When the berserkers entered a room, they dominated it.

Tane strode in, his face set in an emotionless mask. Hemi stood beside him, with a grin on his bearded face. Marin, like most residents of the Enclave, had watched Hemi's dogged pursuit of the sexy female soldier, Camryn, from Squad Nine. The woman had given him the runaround for a while, but they were now a happy couple.

Behind Tane and Hemi came Griff, Dom, and Levi. The three men were talking quietly. Levi, with his trademark man bun, winked at her. Ash brought up the rear.

Marin shivered, but it had nothing to do with fear.

Every time she saw him, she was struck again by how gorgeous he was. He was tall and built, with a movie-star-handsome face, and blue eyes that made her think of turquoise. And that ink that covered both his arms made her want to drool. All those fascinating colors and images. Today, she spotted a bird in flight, soaring high.

Even as her belly tightened, she mentally shook her head. *You're a geek, Marin. He's not for you.* Life had clearly taught her that geek girls did not snag sexy bad boys.

Ash lifted his head and his gaze landed on her. He shot her a smile and her belly flip-flopped.

An absolutely stunning woman breezed in behind the berserkers. Her face was striking rather than beautiful, but she had long, dark hair, and jeans filled out with amazing curves. She walked with a hint of swagger, and oozed confidence. She also had colorful tattoos trailing down her arms, more delicate than Ash's, and mostly vines filled with roses. She was holding a stainless-steel travel mug.

"Hey, where's my coffee?" Levi called out.

Indy Bennett, Squad Three's comms officer, poked out her tongue. "Get your own coffee."

Ash reached out and slung an arm around her neck. "You're mean."

Indy slapped a kiss to his cheek. "Only when it comes to my coffee."

"You're late," Griff muttered.

Indy waggled her brows. "I had a good reason."

Griff scowled. "Which asshole's head do I have to bust, now?"

The woman cocked her hip. "Just because you were my brother's best friend since you could walk, doesn't mean that you're *my* brother, Griff Callan." She spun, heading over to one of the comps. "I'm a big girl, in case you haven't noticed."

The way Griff's gaze fell to Indy's jean-covered ass said he'd definitely noticed.

"I noticed, sweetheart," Ash said with a wink.

Indy blew him a kiss.

Marin shrank back. Of course, Indy was the kind of woman who was perfect for a man like Ash. Sassy, confident, and gorgeous. They'd look beautiful together.

Marin stiffened her spine and shoved her hands in the pockets of her baggy jeans. She couldn't think about that right now. Time to focus on the reason they were here.

AS HOLMES STARTED TALKING, Ash couldn't help but sneak a look at Marin. God, those curls. He watched them bobbing around at the back of her neck. He wanted to sink his hand into them. Feel how soft they were.

"—need to find this data hub," Holmes was saying. "Marin, why don't you tell us exactly what you found?"

Marin stepped forward and cleared her throat. "I found the data on the cubes that your squad found in the creeper breeding ground you destroyed." Her gaze flicked to Ash before moving away. "The information includes references to a central data hub. It seems to be storage for all Gizzida information."

Shit, this was huge. The murmurs of Ash's squad mates rumbled around him.

"So, you mean things like their maps, troop numbers, base locations?" Tane said.

"Everything," Marin answered. "Including other locations around the planet, their strategy, and there are references to a single Gizzida leader. Their queen."

"A queen?" Holmes leaned forward.

"Shit," Noah said, staring at the raptor language on the screen.

This data could turn the tide in their fight.

"But the problem is, I have no idea where the hub is located," Marin continued. "I'm still decoding some of the cubes, but from what we have, I can make some assumptions. The hub would need lots of power, and would be heavily protected."

Tane crossed his muscled arms over his chest. "Yesterday, we went in to investigate a large power spike in the city. There were several raptor patrols in the area."

"There weren't when we were finished," Levi said with a grin.

"True." The corner of Tane's mouth rose. "But we also found something unusual."

"Pulling up the images you took now," Indy said, tapping at a comp.

Ash watched Marin stare up at the images on the big screen on the wall. She tilted her head, concentration on her face. He didn't bother looking at the pictures of the thick, ugly raptor cables. Instead, he looked at her.

Elle stood. "Are they power cables?"

"Could be," Noah said. "If they are, it would mean

this hub is underground." He reached past Elle and tapped on the comp screen. "We need maps of the area—"

Elle elbowed him out of the way, then her fingers flew across the keyboard. "This part of Sydney had lots of offices, and there was a nearby shopping mall." She lifted her head. "There were several underground parking structures."

"And there is the Sydney Advanced Distributor Tunnel System," Tane added.

Elle's eyes widened. "Of course! It would also be really close by." Schematics appeared, showing a massive network of traffic tunnels. "It was built to ease traffic congestion eleven years ago. It's quite possible this data hub could be anywhere in there."

"We need to go in and take a look around," Ash said.

Marin's gaze flicked up to his. For a second, he was caught by clear blue eyes. "That's dangerous. The tunnels are massive."

"It's what we do."

Holmes nodded. "Squad Three, you've been to this area before. I want you to go in. Recon only." A resigned look crossed the man's face. "I guess what I'm really asking is, can you go in and *not* engage the aliens?"

Hemi snorted. "We can do both."

"I'd prefer you didn't warn them. If they think that we're getting close to their hub, they might move it."

"If it is even down there," Niko said.

"We can do it," Tane said.

"I have some tech I've been working on," Marin said.

When all the gazes in the room moved to her, Ash

saw Marin pause. Then she set her shoulders back. "I have a small device that I've invented that can travel autonomously, and will hunt down any comp system to spike into. If it's successful, it can transmit the data to a nearby drone and relay it to us."

"That sounds brilliant, Marin," the general said.

"I haven't tested it in the field yet—"

"Consider this a field test," Holmes said.

"I'll take it in," Ash said.

Tane nodded. "We'll prep to leave in two hours. Can you have it ready by then?"

"Yes." Marin nodded.

As Tane, Hemi, and Indy started to hammer out the mission details, Ash wandered closer to Marin. Her fresh, soapy scent hit him. No perfume for Marin.

She glanced up at him through her eyelashes, watching him cautiously. He liked seeing if he could provoke a reaction, and she was definitely skittish. He wanted so desperately to tell her that he was SuperSoldier3. He wanted her to be as easy with him in real life as she was over the game.

"You're in my personal space," she said tartly.

"I like it here. When can I get this tech of yours?"

"I need to do some more work on it. I need at least an hour." She tucked a curl back.

"Then can you bring it down to the squad locker room just before the mission?" he asked.

She nodded, and sidestepped around him. "Sure. I'd better get to the lab and get to work."

Ash breathed her in. Why the hell was soap and

warm skin such a turn on? "Do I make you nervous, Marin?"

She lifted her chin. "Why would I be nervous?"

He moved closer. "I don't know." He reached out and fingered one of her curls. *So soft.* "So, me touching you doesn't make you nervous?"

She swallowed. "No." A small muscle twitched beside her lush mouth.

"Good. I only like making a woman nervous when I have her naked."

Her eyes boggled. "What?"

He grinned at her. "See you in an hour, or so."

Ash spun to head out of the Command Center. Across the room, he saw Levi watching him and Marin with an interested gaze.

Ash tossed his friend a salute. He had a mission to prep for, and was going to spend it looking forward to the chance to get close to a certain sexy tech genius.

CHAPTER FOUR

Marin watched her tiny spider bot skitter across her desk in the tech lab. It didn't require a controller like a drone. Instead, she'd programmed the bot to be autonomous, with one driving goal—to find the best spot to tap into the Gizzida system.

The bot had six little articulated legs, contained some alien technology, and was covered in scales. It was a blend of human and raptor tech that she'd been working on for months.

And now it was time to deliver it to Ash Connors.

Her stomach turned over and her nerves sprang to life. The man was too...much. Too big, hard, sexy, handsome. She stood and reached for the spider bot. Regardless of all the glorious maleness that was Ash, she'd promised to deliver this to him. The spider bot jumped onto her arm and crawled up. She grabbed it and tucked it in the breast pocket of her checked shirt.

As she walked through the corridors, a few people

called out greetings. Everyone here was going about their lives. Teachers were leading kids down to the classrooms. Men and women sporting toolbelts were heading out to where they were outfitting new living quarters for the intake of new survivors. A smiling couple walked past, hand-in-hand. Off-duty squad members were heading into the games room.

Despite the fact that they were forced to live in hiding underground and were fighting for their survival, the small aspects of life hadn't changed. Kids still grew up and learned, people still worked, ate, and slept. Couples still fell in and out of love, and babies were born. Everyone in the Enclave had their place, and a part to play in keeping their little part of the world functioning.

Marin headed down a ramp and into the corridor where the squad locker rooms were located, right near the Hawk hangars. She found the door with Squad Three written on it, and paused. Someone had taped a rather good sketch of a muscle-bound, tattooed man wrestling with a raptor on it.

From inside, she heard the rumble of male voices. They'd be doing their final preparations for the mission. She gave a brief knock, then pushed the door open.

Just inside the door, she jerked to a halt, her mouth dropping open.

"Hey, Marin," Hemi called out.

She blinked. Hemi was pulling armor on over his black cargo pants. He was wearing a gray T-shirt that was stretched to the absolute limit over his broad, muscled chest. Beside him, Tane was also in black cargo pants, but wasn't wearing a shirt. *Oh. My. God.* She stared at perfectly-formed muscles covered in bronze skin and black ink. His dreadlocks brushed his shoulders, and he lifted his chin at her.

Movement caught her eye, and she managed to drag her gaze off Tane's ridged abdomen. Dom was sitting on a bench, thankfully already dressed in his armor. He was methodically shoving knives into sheaths strapped to his thigh. Griff stood just behind him, also in his armor, and checking a carbine over.

As she glanced past them, her breath caught in her chest, and she was pretty sure her eyes grew to saucer size. Levi was *naked*. He had his back to her, giving her a perfect view of his muscular, tattooed back. It was completely covered in ink. At first, she thought it was some sort of bird, but then she realized it was an angel. A dark, avenging angel with night-black wings.

Of its own accord, her gaze dropped down to a very tight, muscled ass. He half turned, and when he spotted her looking, he grinned at her before pulling his trousers on. As he moved, she caught a wink of metal in his nipple. God, his nipple was pierced.

Suddenly, a big body stepped in front of her, blocking her view of Levi. Dark-green cargo pants rode low on narrow hips. There were hard abs. Sweet Jesus, so many hard abs. Ash had an eight-pack, and Marin took a second to count each contoured ridge of muscle.

Stop staring, Marin. She dragged her gaze up. He had ink on one pec as well, and every inch of him was hard and lean and chiseled.

She felt a rush of dampness between her thighs.

Clearing her throat, she looked at his face. He was scowling.

"You have the tech?"

She nodded. He was probably pissed at her for staring at him like a sex-deprived hussy. "Ah...I need..." *What the hell did she need?* Marin couldn't seem to get her brain firing. She saw Levi shift into view behind Ash. He had clothes on now, and was tying his hair back.

Ash sidestepped and blocked her view of Levi again. "You need what?"

"Huh?" *God, get it together, Marin. You aren't a trembling virgin.* "I need..." Her gaze drifted down again. "You to put a shirt on."

Chuckles sounded, and Marin felt heat in her cheeks. One of Ash's eyebrows rose in a flash of amusement. He leaned over, grabbed a T-shirt, and yanked it on.

Finally, she got her brain cells functioning. "I'll need to give you some instructions about the spider bot."

He nodded and gripped her arm. Marin's brain cells blissed out again. There was so much strength in that grip, and she saw his hands were scarred. This was a man of action, who wasn't afraid to fight, and stand between people and danger.

Ash pulled her out of the locker room. As he strode down the hall, she had to work hard to keep up with his long stride.

"You enjoy the view?" His voice was sharp.

Right, he was pissed she'd looked at him. "Um. I'm not going to apologize for being female."

He grunted.

Well, Marin would have been mortified if he'd seen

her undressed. "I'm sorry, Ash. I didn't even think you'd still be getting dressed. I'm sorry I stared at you."

He glanced at her sharply. "I was dressed."

She tried to look solemn. "No, you weren't. You didn't have your shirt on and I saw that you have an eight-pack. And a tiny mole beside your navel." *Oh, God, stop talking Marin.* But she couldn't help the babbling. "You must have very low body fat."

A flash of amusement crept into his blue gaze. "Levi was naked."

"He was?" All she could see in her head was Ash's bare chest.

"Yeah."

She frowned. "Right. He was. I'm sorry I saw him naked."

"He won't care." Ash's scowl reappeared. "He probably liked it."

"I should have knocked louder."

Ash just shook his head, and led her through a large doorway.

The Hawk hangar was a huge, cavernous space filled with coverall-covered maintenance people bustling between the Hawk quadcopters. Marin loved the quadcopters. They were such a great design, and perfect for getting the squads in and out of missions. They'd lost a few since the start of the fight against the Gizzida, and the maintenance team were very protective of the remaining aircraft.

Ash pulled her over to where some crates were stacked against the wall. He gestured for her to sit and then sat across from her. He hitched a leg up and his thigh brushed hers. Marin worked hard to keep her brain from drifting back into drooling mode.

"Where's the bot?" he asked.

Marin pulled the spider bot out of her pocket and held her palm up.

He leaned forward, interest igniting in his eyes. "It's a spider."

She nodded. "I designed it based on a spider's physiology. It's an autonomous bot, so he'll travel himself, tracking down any signal he detects from the raptor system. Then he'll find the best place to spike in." The bot skittered up her forearm. Ash held out a hand, his fingers brushing hers, and the bot leaped across from her arm to his hand. She felt a spike of heat where their skin touched.

"This is amazing, Marin."

"Thanks." Heat filled her cheeks. "So you just need to get close enough, then it'll do the rest."

"Got it."

She showed him how to deactivate the small bot and he tucked it away. Then his gaze met hers and he tilted his head. "I have a question for you."

She shifted on the box. "Okay," she said, suspiciously.

"When I get back, do you want to grab a drink?"

Marin blinked. "A drink?"

He smiled "A drink. A cold beverage."

She frowned. "You mean with the berserkers? To celebrate the mission?"

"No. Just you and me. The two of us."

Marin frowned. Where did this come from? Was he making fun of her? "Are you playing me?"

His eyebrows rose. "No."

She narrowed her gaze. "Why do you want to have a drink with me?"

He leaned closer and his scent hit her. Something dark and sexy. Her pulse spiked.

He smiled at her again. "I think you know why, Marin."

ASH LOVED WATCHING the little crease appear in the middle of Marin's brow.

"No, I don't," she answered.

"Yes, you do."

She blinked. "Then it's a no."

He straightened. That wasn't the answer he'd been anticipating. "No?"

She waved a hand in the air. "Guys like you, do not have drinks with women like me."

"Women like you?" He wasn't sure where she was going with this. And to be frank, he wasn't used to women saying no to him.

She shook her head, her curls bouncing. "You need a woman like Indy. Sexy and confident."

"Indy is a friend. She's like a sister to me."

Marin leaned forward, like she was imparting a state secret. "Ash, I'm a geek."

"I know. A smart and sexy geek. I like it."

She froze. "You do?"

"Yes."

Then she shook her head. "No. Handsome biker bad boys do not find geeks sexy."

"I do. I like smart, funny, and fresh."

"You'd find it interesting at first. You'd think I was funny or cute. But then you'll decide I get lost in my work and don't give you enough attention. Or that I need to talk and smile more. Or dress sexier. Or I'll say something that makes you feel dumb." Her eyes widened. "Which you're not."

"Marin." He reached out and grabbed her hand. "Don't judge me by the dickheads you've dealt with in your past."

He watched her mouth drop open, then click shut. She stared at him, and he could almost hear that clever brain of hers ticking over.

"I like you. I'd like to grab a drink with you." *Then strip you naked and lick you all over.* Something told him she wasn't quite ready to hear that, yet.

She shook her head again, and he was mesmerized by the bobbing curls.

"It'll start with a drink, then you'll break my heart and stomp on the shattered pieces. I'm not equipped to deal with you."

Ash started to laugh, but when he realized she was serious he bit it back and sobered. "Don't say that. I'm the one who's out of your league. You're smart and brilliant. I went to college for a grand total of eight months. I bet you have more than one degree."

"Three. But that's beside the point. I'm—" she looked down at their joined hands "—I'm not brave enough."

Ash had seen enough bad in his life to recognize good

when he saw it. "Yes, you are. We both know you're fiercer than you give yourself credit for, Princess."

His words fell between them and Marin froze like a stone. Her wide eyes glued to his face, and then something flickered in them. "SuperSoldier3?" Her voice was a whisper.

Shit. He'd given himself away. "Marin—"

She shot to her feet. "*You're* SuperSoldier3?"

He held out a hand to her. This wasn't how he'd wanted to reveal himself, right before a mission. "Marin—"

"Oh, God." Her cheeks turned pink, and she glanced around wildly. "I thought you were someone off the *tech* team, not a *berserker*." She was breathing fast now, her chest rising and falling.

Ash grabbed her hips and pulled her between his outstretched legs. "Breathe, Marin."

"This is...is..." She closed her eyes, her face growing pale. "I told you things." Then her eyes snapped open. "Oh, God, I touched—" She broke off.

"You touched yourself." He pulled her closer when she tried to yank away. "And it was sexy as hell, Marin. I touched myself while I imagined what you were doing. Came harder than I ever have before."

Her lips parted, and his gaze slid to them. Shit, she was so cute.

"This can't be happening," she murmured.

"Marin."

"This is a joke, right? Make fun of Marin Mitchell." She arched her neck, looking around. "Are your squad mates going to jump out and have a laugh?"

"No." Anger fired. "I told you not to judge me by the assholes you've dealt with before."

Her eyes glinted. "The assholes in school or college, or the assholes when I started work? There have been plenty of them."

Damn, he'd fucking screwed this up, big time.

"I won't be the butt of anyone's joke." She yanked away from him.

Ash surged to his feet. "I told you, I'm not making fun of you. This is—"

"And I told you, I know the rules of the world. Men like you do not end up with women like me." She spun to stalk out.

He grabbed the back of her shirt, and held her in place. Damn, he didn't have time to sort this out right now, and he hated seeing her go like this. "I have to be on a Hawk in twenty minutes. But I want you to think about the fact that I don't give a fuck about anyone's stupid rules."

She froze and looked at him over her shoulder.

"I didn't care about following the rules before the invasion, and I sure as hell don't now." He used her shirt to reel her in closer.

She struggled for a second and Ash reached around, gripped her jaw, and tilted it up to him. As soon as his lips touched hers, she went still. Then she opened her mouth and a moan vibrated deep in her throat.

So damn sweet. Ash plunged his tongue into her mouth, drinking in the taste of her. She spun, her hands sinking into his shirt and kissed him back. She pressed up against him, making hungry little noises in her throat.

Damn, he needed more time. Which he didn't have. He'd never suspected that Marin was hiding a wild side under her checked shirts and curls.

He deepened the kiss, making it long, wet, and hard, before he lifted his head. "Shit, Marin, I'm hard as a rock. That kiss just about blew my head off."

Marin stumbled back, lifting a hand to touch her kiss-swollen lips. "That...I..." she paused, dragging in a breath. "That shouldn't have happened."

"Bullshit. It happened and is going to happen again."

She straightened, that stubborn look coming back into her face. "Ash, I like fitting things in the right place. I like rules—"

"And I like to break them." He stepped closer, until only an inch separated them, and lowered his head until he felt the flutter of her warm breath on his cheek. Fuck, he wanted to kiss her again. "I have to go, but when I get back, I'm coming to find you, Princess."

CHAPTER FIVE

M arin stood at the back of the Command Center, trying not to fidget.

Around her, the quiet hubbub of activity barely registered. Her gaze was glued to the camera feed on the screen on the wall. It was from a helmet cam, and showed the inside of a Hawk. The quadcopter was speeding toward alien territory.

She was still in shock about Ash's revelation. Her brain still wasn't willing to accept the information, and shied away from the thought of him being SuperSoldier3. She twisted her hands together.

Ash Connors was SuperSoldier3. *Her* SuperSoldier3.

And he'd kissed her. And boy, the man could *kiss*.

Her gaze fell on Indy, who was seated behind a comp and looked completely composed. The tattooed woman was drinking coffee from a huge mug. How could she be so relaxed, knowing her friends were headed into danger?

The general stood quietly to the side, his hands clasped behind his back. Noah was leaning against a table, eating an apple.

God, Marin's nerves were making her feel sick. That, along with knowing she'd had online nookie with *Ash Connors*.

Don't forget the hard, hungry kiss that left you damp, needy, and tingly.

Great. All she needed was her inner hussy reminding her of every little, sexy detail.

On the Hawk, the berserkers were talking and joking. They were heading into alien territory, but didn't show a shred of fear. Marin didn't know how they did it.

Her gaze found Ash and flutters started up in her belly. Her gaze traced the line of his strong jaw. Why did he have to be so handsome?

"Nearly at the touchdown point," came a deep male voice. She knew it was Finn Erickson, the Hawk pilot.

Marin's nerves were stretched tight. Ash was Super-Soldier3. *Jeez.* She squeezed her eyes shut, her stomach churning. She still couldn't quite believe it. Maybe if she ignored it, it just wouldn't be true. A girl could dream.

"Oh, those berserkers."

A woman's low murmur made Marin look over. Two Command Center technicians were talking to each other nearby.

"Big, bad, and tattooed," the other woman said with a sigh.

"I've been trying to get Ash Connors into my bed for *weeks*."

"I hear he loves going down on women. He can go *all* night."

Marin stared hard at the screen, her cheeks and her ears burning. She did not want to think of Ash with other women. Or what he did with those other women. On the screen, she watched the Hawk start to descend. She edged closer to Indy. The woman was leaning forward now, monitoring drone feed of the area.

The quadcopter halted a few meters above the ground. Tane pulled the side door open and in the Hawk, the berserkers flicked on their illusion armor. The illusion systems were designed to camouflage by blurring them on visual, distorting sounds, and jamming sensors. One by one, the soldiers all flickered out of existence.

"How do you keep track of them?" Marin asked, curious.

Indy didn't look up. "Like this." She touched something on her comp. On the screen, a ghostly outline of each berserker appeared. "I have a special filter that lets me see them."

One after another, the men leaped out of the Hawk with powerful, athletic moves. Marin easily picked out Ash's tall, lean form.

This was a bad idea. She shouldn't be in here, watching the man who'd lied to her. Who'd played the worst kind of deception with her. It wasn't the first time. She'd had all kinds of idiots play practical jokes on her at school. She'd been smart, late to develop, and preferred reading to socializing. She'd been an easy target. At least she'd had some good friends, and mostly hadn't let any of the teasing worry her.

Marin blew out a breath. She wasn't an awkward teen anymore. She was a woman, and while she might not have Indy's swagger or Claudia's toughness, she was smart, and good at what she did. She'd even had an okay sex life prior to the invasion. Nothing to compose sonnets over, but decent.

"Approaching tunnel entrance." Tane's cool voice. "Heading in."

The screen displayed a four-lane road, heading down into a tunnel. The pavement was cracked in places, and several smashed and overturned cars were piled up, off to one side.

The berserkers were quiet, moving as a tight group, as they approached the tunnel.

A guttural grunting sounded, and the squad froze. A raptor patrol sauntered out of the tunnel, ugly scaled weapons clasped in their clawed hands. Their heavy boots thumped on the pavement.

Marin's short nails dug into her palms. She watched the berserkers crouch by the cars. God, one wrong move, and the raptors would trip over them.

After what felt like an eternity, the raptor patrol moved on and out of range.

"Squad Three, you are clear to move," Indy said. "I don't have any drone coverage once you enter the tunnel, so you'll be on your own. I should continue to have comms, unless you go too deep underground."

"Night vision on," Tane murmured. The berserkers all flipped night vision devices over their left eyes, and moved forward.

Marin watched intently. This was a side of the

berserkers people rarely saw. Everyone usually saw them drinking and having fun, or heard about their wild fights. No one talked about the skill or focus that was on display right now.

Squad Three passed through the arch of the tunnel, under some speed limit signs hanging drunkenly off the stone from rusted bolts.

Marin's nerves were so tight she could barely breathe, but she couldn't look away. The squad moved through the wide tunnel in close formation. For all their wildness, she could see they were a good squad, and she knew they always got the job done.

They descended down a ramp, and ahead, the road was littered with more destroyed cars. Everything was still and quiet. It was spooky.

Ahead, the tunnel split, and the grunting, guttural language of the raptors echoed through the stillness.

"Keep quiet, and keep moving," Indy murmured. "Follow the power signature and look for those ugly-ass cables."

They took the left-hand tunnel, and then paused when they came to a door. The lettering was faded, but Marin could still make out the word *Maintenance*. Dom stepped forward and did something to the lock. The door popped open and the berserkers slipped through it.

Inside, the tunnel was small, only wide enough for single file. The walls were lined with electrical panels. They moved down it, and then Tane carefully opened another door at the end. As he looked out into another vehicle tunnel, Marin hissed.

A large, alien cable glowed red in the darkness. It

stretched out in front of them, disappearing into the blackness in both directions.

"That looks like a good place to let the spider bot go," Marin said.

Indy relayed the message, and Ash pulled the bot from his pocket.

Marin looked at her creation on the screen, and crossed her fingers. "Do your thing, little guy." She held her breath. She was excited to see what her bot could do.

Ash stepped forward, and set the bot down near the cable. It turned in a circle, then carefully lifted two legs. She knew it was sensing the environment around it.

Then it leaped up on the cable, illuminated by the red light, before it leaped off the other side and scuttled off into the darkness.

Go, little guy.

The berserkers reversed course, moving back through the maintenance tunnel.

"Any idea what the raptors are doing in there?" Holmes said.

Indy shook her head. "Lots of patrols." She leaned forward. "Look over there."

There was a line of huge shadows against one side of the tunnel the squad was moving through. Marin sucked in a breath. They were all the squat, black vehicles the aliens used. Big and rugged, with spikes mounted on the front.

"Looks like they're using the place for storage," Indy said.

"Heading out now," Tane whispered.

"Think the hub's in there?" Noah asked.

Marin wondered what her spider bot was doing. "It's likely." She really hoped so.

"Fuck."

She stiffened, her eyes flashing to the screen. That was Ash's voice.

The view on the screen switched to the camera on Ash's helmet. He was to the far left of his group, near the entrance to a side tunnel. Marin watched as a huge raptor appeared out of the darkness. It was headed right toward Ash.

"Move slowly," Tane whispered.

Ash backed up, but the raptor was striding at a fast pace. It stepped inside the illusion from Ash's armor.

The ugly beast looked shocked, his red eyes wide in his reptilian face. To him, it would have looked like Ash had appeared out of thin air. Ash shot forward, a large knife in his hand. He slammed into the alien. The two scuffled.

The view changed back to Tane's camera. Marin watched Ash and the raptor swing around, straining against each other. Ash's arm moved fast, thrusting with his blade. *Come on, Ash.* She knew how close they were to getting out of there.

If the raptor called for help or they made too much noise, the berserkers would be discovered.

Finally, the raptor fell backward, slamming to the floor. Ash rose, chest heaving, and wiped his combat knife clean.

Marin let out a shaky breath. Her hands were trembling.

"Hide the body," Tane said quietly. "Back in the maintenance tunnel."

Ash nodded. Levi moved with him, and they each grabbed one of the raptor's arms. The men dragged the huge alien toward the small doorway.

Levi wedged the door open, and with a few grunts and heaves, they shoved the raptor's body into the space and closed the door.

The berserkers moved fast, sticking close to the wall. Soon, they were jogging back up the ramp to the upper tunnel. A moment later, they stepped outside into the sunshine.

Marin's shoulders sagged. Indy looked calm as she swiped the screen. Marin knew she'd never be able to be on a squad, or even be a comms officer.

"Hawk incoming," Indy said.

The berserkers moved fast now, less concerned about noise. They ran through a street, across an overgrown park, and into a parking lot attached to the hulking shadow of a former shopping mall. When Marin saw the Hawk descending to pick them up, she finally managed to take her first full, deep breath.

Tane waved his team aboard. "Coming home."

Marin watched as they all settled in, retracting their helmets, and stowing their carbines.

"I need a beer," Hemi said.

"I want tequila," Levi called out. "A lot of it. Fuck, Ash. When that raptor just about stepped on you..." Levi shook his head. "I'll buy the first round."

Ash looked up at the camera in the Hawk. "I have something I need to do."

Marin shivered, her fingernails digging into her thighs.

"You planning to play that pansy-assed game with the geeks?" Levi laughed. "Your cock's going to fall off."

Marin stiffened. They were ribbing him for playing the game. A bad taste filled her mouth. His friends were already giving him hell, and before long, he'd start playing less, and not want anything to do with it. Or the people who played it. Marin knew this story very well.

She had no right to be doing anything with Ash Connors. The two of them together made no sense, and Marin liked it when the world made sense. When she was in her own comfortable little place.

She stood. "I need to get back to the tech lab, and check what the spider bot is doing." She escaped the Command Center, with one final glance at the screen. Ash was in profile, smiling, one tattooed arm on display.

Better yet, she'd take her portable comp and find a quiet place to spend the next few hours. Alone.

ASH STEPPED out of the shower, swiping his towel over his wet hair. He felt edgy as hell.

He knew what he wanted. Or, rather, who he wanted.

As soon as he'd returned from the mission, he'd looked for Marin. She was nowhere to be found. She hadn't been in the tech lab, her room, the Command Center, or the dining room.

Dammit. Naked, he sat down in front of his

computer. He knew a Pre-Emptive Strike game was starting. She never missed a game. He logged in and waited for PrincessBadass to appear.

And waited. And waited.

Fuck. Ash kicked the leg of the desk, and then stabbed the key to log off.

He'd fucked up. She'd told him about growing up and not feeling like she fit in. He knew Marin was skittish, even a touch innocent. And he was a ham-fisted biker and about as subtle as a freight train.

He pulled on some jeans and a T-shirt, and shoved his feet into his boots, then slammed out of his room. Moments later, he strode into a smaller hangar bay just off the main Hawk hangar. This was where the Z6-Hunters were stored. He took in the row of Hunters gleaming under the lights.

The armor-plated personnel carriers were black and sleek, and had rugged tires and deadly autocannons mounted on top.

There was a clang of metal on metal, followed by a curse. Ash rounded the Hunters and spotted Levi in one corner, working on one of the modified bikes that the berserkers had built. Levi had grease smeared on his white T-shirt, and his long hair was out, brushing his shoulders.

"Thought you had a date with a bottle of tequila?"

"Hey." Levi nodded his head at some nearby crates. An open bottle of tequila rested on top. "I wanted to do some work on my bike."

Ash knew his friend well. Working on bikes or cars was Levi's escape. In the Iron Kings, Levi had been known as Gears, and made the club a hell of a lot of money with his rebuilds of classic cars. Ash had been called Doc. Neither of them used those names anymore. Gears and Doc had been left behind in the ashes of their bombed-out clubhouse and their dead brothers.

The berserker bikes were big and rugged, and covered in modifications. They'd been made to ride out on missions, and had armor-plating and missile launchers added, as well as a few other surprises.

"Thought you had a war game tonight." Levi waggled his eyebrows.

At the mention of Pre-Emptive Strike, Ash grabbed the tequila and took a huge swig. The alcohol was a pleasant burn down his throat. "Nope."

Levi snatched up a rag and wiped his hands, eyeing Ash. "Only one thing puts that look on a man's face."

"I'm fine."

"A woman," Levi continued.

"Don't want to talk about it." And he didn't want to wonder where the hell Marin was.

Levi leaned back over the black bike. "Sure?"

"She's too good for me anyway. Smart and sweet. She took one look at me and freaked."

Levi's head jerked up. "Fuck off, Connors. You're a good guy. And you're smart as hell, even though you hide it."

"Thanks, bro." Ash snatched up some tools and moved over to his bike. He set to work taking the side panel off. He may as well do something to keep his mind off things.

They worked in silence for a while. This was how it had

always been between the two of them, easy. Knowing they each had the other's backs. That didn't mean they hadn't traded a few punches or called each other out sometimes. But that was part of friendship, too, knowing they could fight and speak the truth to each other, but still be friends.

Ash was lying on his side, tightening some lines in his bike's engine, when he noticed Levi eyeing the Hunters. One of the vehicles had its hood up. Clearly, someone was working on it.

"Heard they were doing some upgrades." Levi shoved his rag in the back pocket of his jeans and strode over to the Hunter. "I want to take a little look." He leaned over, poking around under the hood.

Ash snorted. "Remember, you get testy if someone pokes around in your engines."

"No one here to see."

But a few minutes later, a female voice echoed through the hangar. "Hey! Hands off, biker man."

Levi jerked upright and Ash sat up. A redhead—with killer curves packed into jeans and a form-fitting green T-shirt that showed off her assets—was striding across the space. She was also holding a wrench in her hand and had a grease stain on one cheek. Her brow was creased and she was glaring at Levi.

Chrissy was a recent survivor who'd joined the Enclave. The auburn-haired woman had been held in alien captivity, and been rescued by Devlin Gray from the intel team, and kickass Taylor Cates from Squad Nine.

"Just looking, sweet thing," Levi said with a grin.

"Don't 'sweet thing' me." She got close and pointed the wrench at him. "I've been working my butt off on this Hunter. I don't need you messing it up."

"I know a few things about engines," Levi said.

She glared daggers at him. "I'm a qualified mechanic. I don't need any help." She bumped the wrench into Levi's chest. "Hands off."

Levi lifted his palms up in surrender.

Chrissy sniffed and turned back to the Hunter. A second later, Levi moved in close behind and murmured something.

Ash was too far away to hear what Levi whispered, but suddenly Chrissy turned and swung the wrench at his head. Luckily, Levi had fast reflexes.

He ducked and laughed. "I like a woman with attitude. Suspected you had some hidden under that red hair, Spitfire."

"Out of my way, biker man." She shot him a fake-sweet smile. "Or I'll show you attitude and I guarantee you won't like it."

As Chrissy stormed out of the hangar, Levi watched her with a smile on his face.

Ash knew that look. When Levi wanted something, he let nothing get in his way.

"Don't think she's receptive, brother," Ash said.

Levi's smile sharpened. "She will be." He moved back to his bike, but his gaze was on Ash. "I've always believed that when you see something you want, you go in guns blazing after it." He glanced back in the direction where Chrissy disappeared. "Or her."

Ash considered his friend's words, and thought of Marin.

"She worth it?" Levi asked quietly.

Ash knew Levi wasn't talking about Chrissy. Ash's head filled with an image of sunny curls and glasses perched on a cute nose. "Yeah."

Levi picked up another tool and went back to work on his bike. "World's a fucked-up place these days, Ash. There's not too much good left in it, so when you find some, you grab the fuck on and don't let go. Don't let anything get in the way of you taking a little piece of it and protecting it."

"You're pretty smart for a rough-as-guts biker," Ash said.

Levi smiled. "Get out of here."

Ash stood and wiped his hands. He decided to follow his best friend's advice.

CHAPTER SIX

Marin sat alone in the tech lab. It was late, so the main lights were off, and she just had a lamp on to illuminate her desk.

She'd hung out in the pool, of all places, with her portable comp until she was sure Ash would have given up looking for her. *Coward, thy name is Marin.* She sighed. She'd missed playing Pre-Emptive Strike, and because of the humidity in the pool room, her hair had turned all kinds of crazy.

She pushed the unruly mass off her face and forced herself to focus on the code on the screen. She wanted the sweet oblivion of work, so she could studiously ignore the fact that the sexiest man in base had been tricking her into touching herself while they played a computer game together.

Ugh. Marin let her head fall forward and clunk her desk. She was so embarrassed. The more she thought about it, the more she knew that Ash must be laughing at her behind her back. Tease the geek girl, then laugh about it with your friends. She sat up and shook her head. *It isn't high school anymore, Marin.* He was probably in bed with some nameless, faceless, gorgeous woman, and not even thinking about Marin Mitchell. God, Marin hated that woman, whoever she was.

She tapped the screen to check on the spider bot. She frowned. No contact. She was sure it should have found somewhere to spike into the alien system by now. She tapped her fingers on her desk. What if it had been found by the raptors? Or damaged? Or flat out didn't work?

A notification pinged up on her screen. Hmm, one of the servers needed a visual check in the comp system server room. She touched the screen, tucked her portable comp under her arm, and then pushed out of the lab.

The server room wasn't far. She often snuck in there to work, when she needed to get away from the chaos of the tech lab.

"Marin."

Uh-oh. She spun and saw Ash storming down the corridor toward her.

Her heart jumped at the savage look on his face. God, she wasn't sure she was ready to deal with him yet. She spun and walked down the hall at a fast clip.

Without thinking, she ducked down a side corridor. He'd never find her server room. When she took the next corridor, she was half running.

"Marin!"

He was gaining on her. Chest heaving, she turned another corner, and saw the secure door for the server room.

She slapped her palm to the electronic lock. It beeped, and she wrenched the door open.

But before she could close it, a tattooed arm shoved past her and slammed the door wide again.

Ash's big body pressed up against her. He nudged her inside and banged the door closed behind them, locking them in the server room. Her portable comp dropped to the floor with a *slap*.

The space was filled with several rows of small, slim-line servers. Lights blinked on the units, and there was a quiet hum in the air. The desk she sometimes used was on the far side of the room, pushed up against the wall.

"You hiding from me?"

"Um...no. I..." She couldn't even string any words together in his presence. *Great.*

He moved closer, backing her up against one line of servers. "You know you have a tell."

She frowned. "A tell?"

He nodded. "When you lie, a muscle beside your mouth twitches."

Marin reached up to touch the corner of her mouth. "It does not."

"It twitched again."

She dragged in a deep breath. "Look, Ash. Can we just forget everything, never discuss...our game playing, and never see each other again?" Otherwise Marin was going to have to consider moving to Mongolia. Although, she was pretty sure the Gizzida were there, too.

"Hell, no." He pressed his hands on either side of her, caging her in. Her gaze fell on all those yummy tattoos.

No, Marin. Don't look at his tattoos. Or the hard muscles beneath them.

"We've been having fun," Ash said. "I want more of that."

She stared at him. "We do not work."

"We do."

"I'm not interested."

He smiled. "That cute little muscle twitched again."

"You had your laugh," she said. "I'm sure you've been laughing yourself silly at...playing me and me not knowing who you were—"

He leaned closer. "There's nothing silly about you. You're sexy as hell. I've been watching you for a long time, Marin. I wasn't sure you'd want a guy like me, so I thought I'd take it slow. Things just got out of hand before I could tell you who I was."

She blinked. "A guy like you? A sexy, badass guy who can have any woman he wants?"

"And I'm telling you I want you, but you aren't listening." He tilted his head. "I'm the kind of guy who takes what he wants. Who claims a woman and demands everything from her."

Marin's breath hitched. "Everything?"

"Everything."

She shook her head. "You've had your joke—"

He went tense and she felt the air turn charged. "This isn't a joke," he said firmly. "Look down."

She stared into his eyes for a second before she looked down. Heat filled her cheeks. She could hardly miss the bulge straining the zipper of his jeans. The really huge bulge.

She jerked her gaze back up. "Ash..."

"I'm just a man, Marin. I bleed red like you. I laugh like you. I feel like you."

His words echoed through her.

"I told you things I've never told anyone. About going to college and how fucking disappointed I was when I had to leave." He sucked in a breath. "I was studying medicine. Wanted to be a doctor."

Medicine? She knew that was a tough course.

"I wanted to help people. Instead, I was sucked back into the club, the Iron Kings. Tried to help my dad. Tried to help my sister, until I found her dead from an overdose."

God. She could imagine him...yanked from studying, the campus parties, the pretty cheerleaders.

He looked at the floor. "Life doesn't ever let me have anything good."

His quiet words hit her under her heart. "I told you my secrets, too. You know why I can't quite make myself believe you want me."

He sank a hand into her curls and tilted her head back. "Then I'll have to prove it to you."

"Oh." Her voice was husky. She licked her lips.

Ash groaned. "Marin. I want you. You going to let me taste you?"

She pressed her hands to his chest, her fingers digging into his shirt. "This can't be happening."

"I don't usually ask a woman for permission."

She made a sound. "Because they're throwing themselves at you?"

His lips quirked. "Maybe. So, you ready?"

The air thickened. Right now, Marin could only think about Ash and the emotions swirling around inside her. "Yes."

"Thank fuck." He tugged her the last few inches and pressed his mouth to hers. She absorbed the impact of those firm lips moving over hers. Then she moaned and opened her mouth, and Ash was done being polite.

His kiss was hard and when her lips parted, his tongue thrust into her mouth. *Oh. God.* Every thought rushed out of Marin's head, and she lost herself in the sensations.

Soon, she was pressed hard against his muscled body, practically climbing him, her hands clenched on his shoulders. He changed the angle, deepening the kiss, his tongue sliding against hers.

"Damn, sweetheart." He tugged her head back, his mouth moving down her neck, nipping at her skin. "You go wild when I touch you."

She ran a hand down his arm and got sidetracked by his tattoos. She traced over the fascinating images—a snarling dog, a fierce dragon, patterns that looked like feathers and scales.

"Do you like them?" he asked quietly.

She looked up and nodded. "I see something different every time. And they look sexy."

"Touch them." His voice deepened.

She did, tracing her fingers over each design. But she was more conscious of the hard, warm man beneath the ink. "I have no experience with a man like you."

"Good." He backed her up and she felt the edge of the desk hit her butt.

"What are you doing?" she asked.

"Told you I needed a taste of you, Princess."

"You just kissed me—"

"That's not where I want to taste you."

Her breath hitched. *Oh.* Desire was a hot coil in her belly.

He gripped her hips, and with one flex of his arms, he lifted her onto the desk. She heard something fall to the floor, but she couldn't be bothered to look. She stared into his blue-green eyes, and he cupped her jaw and kissed her again.

Sweet Jesus. She moaned, and his tongue slid deep. His hand buried itself in her hair, pulling just hard enough to make it feel so good. Lost, Marin lifted a leg and wrapped it around his hip.

She needed him. She needed everything.

All of a sudden, he pulled back and Marin let out a cry of protest. He dropped into the battered desk chair. Her gaze dropped to the bulge in the front of his jeans. God, it was so big. She wondered what it would look like. What it would feel like if he—

Ash groaned. "I can see everything you're thinking in your eyes."

She licked her lips, feeling a rush of moisture between her thighs. "You can?"

"You want to see my cock, sweetheart?"

"Yes," she breathed.

"What else do you want?"

"I want...to touch it. Taste it."

Another groan. "Another time. Not today. Today, is all about you."

His hands went to her leggings, tugging them downward.

"Ash—?"

He pushed her shoes off, and pulled her leggings off her legs. "Right now, I'm going to put my mouth between your legs."

She sucked in a shaky breath. "Okay."

He slid a finger under the edge of her soaked panties. Then, he ripped them off. Marin's belly spasmed. No one had ever torn her clothes off before.

His gaze was hot on her. "So fucking pretty and pink, Marin. Now, I'm going to eat you until you scream."

Oh. God. Marin gripped the edge of the desk and watched his dark head lower between her legs. She quivered, sure she might come just watching him.

She felt the brush of his stubble on her inner thighs, and then his tongue slid through her folds. Her moan tangled with his groan. He pressed a hand to her belly and held her still, his mouth moving with sucks and licks that had her squirming.

"Holy cow, Ash." Her orgasm was already bearing down on her. She'd never come this fast before.

"Taste so good." He licked her again, his tongue stabbing inside her. His lips circled her clit and her hips lifted. Her cries echoed off the rows of servers and she sank her hands into his hair.

"Love those sweet sounds."

"Ash." Her voice trembled.

"Come, Princess. Come hard on my tongue."

When he sucked her clit again, her climax slammed

into her. She screamed his name, her fingers twisting in his hair.

Ash lifted his head, satisfaction on his face. "Again."

Marin's eyes widened. He couldn't mean...? "Again?"

His hand slid up her thigh, and a long finger thrust inside her. Marin threw her head back. He slid a second finger inside her, stretching her.

"Tight. You'll feel so damn good stretched around my cock."

"I...I won't come again," she panted.

"You sure?"

"I never have."

His smile was slow and he pulled his fingers out of her. "Then let's see. First, I want to watch you taste yourself."

Her mouth formed an *O*. A part of Marin's orgasm-fuzzy brain could still hardly believe she was half naked, with Ash Connors' mouth and hands between her legs.

His fingers brushed over her lips and she licked out with her tongue. His gaze was glued there, a hungry look on his face.

Feeling bolder, she sucked one of his fingers into her mouth, tasting her own musk.

"Shit," he muttered. "I'm gonna blow my load in my trousers, which I've never done before, if you don't stop that." He nudged her back and lowered his head again. Two fingers slid back inside her, and as he worked them in and out of her, his clever mouth found her clit again.

Marin cried out and let herself drown in the sensations.

ASH COULD GET ADDICTED to the taste of Marin Mitchell.

He kept licking and sucking, loving every sound she made. He loved watching what a woman liked, and he loved driving them wild. But with Marin, he saw the shocked delight under her pleasure, and he knew he was taking her places she'd never been before.

There was no pretense with Marin. She wasn't here with him because she was after something, or just wanted to get off, or bag a berserker. She was smart, pretty, and despite her protests, fierce in her own way.

Ash would never get enough of her. Her sweet cries echoed in his ears, and as her second orgasm hit, shock and pleasure skittered over her face.

She came hard, throwing her head back, her sweet, curvy body shaking. Ash lifted his head, looking at her sprawled on the desk, half naked, her hair in disarray and her chest quickly rising and falling.

So damn sexy.

He leaned down and nipped at her thigh. "Sweet and sexy Marin."

Her eyes were a little dazed. "No one's thought so before." Her voice was huskier than usual.

Every man before him had been an idiot. He helped her sit up, stroking her smooth skin.

Her gaze dropped to his cock. "Um, do you want—?"

His fingers tightened on her thighs. "Yes. Hell, yes. But I want more than a rushed quickie the first time I slide my cock inside you."

She nodded, heat in her gaze.

"I'm tired of jacking off, imagining I'm coming inside you instead of my hand."

She moaned. "Ash, I want you."

Suddenly, a loud chime sounded and Marin froze.

Ash groaned. "That had better be something important."

"The spider bot made contact!" She scrambled off the desk, then she looked down. "I'm naked! I can't concentrate on anything like this."

Ash grabbed her leggings and gently pulled them back up her legs, settling them in place, followed by her shoes. She stood there watching him. He snatched up the torn, lace-edged panties and stuffed them in his pocket. What he really wanted to do was drag her into his bed and keep her there for days.

She hurried over and scooped her portable comp off the floor. She tapped madly at the screen.

"The bot is in!" She grinned at him.

Ash had never seen anything as beautiful as that smile.

She stared at the screen and he watched data fill it, all in the raptor language. Within seconds, she was muttering to herself, completely absorbed.

"I should feel put out about the fact you've forgotten I'm even here," he said.

She straightened and eyed him warily. "Sorry."

"I'm not angry, Marin. What are you doing?"

"The spider bot's linked in." Excitement filled her face. "It's transmitting data, but it's got heavy encryption." She cracked her knuckles. "But I'm certain I can get through it."

"And then we'll have access to the Gizzida's data."

"That's the plan."

He reached for the battered desk chair and spun it toward her. "Then get to work, Princess."

Marin sat and started tapping. She reached into a pocket and pulled her glasses on. Ash almost groaned. She looked so fucking cute in her glasses. He planned to fuck her with them on one day.

It didn't take her long to get lost in her work again. Ash smiled and leaned against the wall. Hell, he could watch her do this all night. Especially since he still had the taste of her on his lips.

"Dammit, this encryption is tough." She tossed the comp onto the desk. She tilted her head to one side and then the other, working out the kinks.

"You'll work it out."

His voice startled her and she blinked. "Oh. I thought you'd left. Uh, this must be so boring for you."

He smiled at her again. "I could watch you work all night. You get this sexy little crease in your brow when you're concentrating. And you bounce in your seat when things are going well."

She blinked. "No one's ever watched me work before. Or thought I looked sexy doing it." She tucked some of her curls back. "None of my usual tricks were working. I've set up some things to try and break the alien encryption. But it could take hours, or days." She huffed out a frustrated breath. "Hell, even years."

"Give it a chance. You designed it, so I bet it'll get

through eventually."

Her cheeks turned pink. "I need to update the general." She tapped out a message on her comp. A second later, it beeped with a response. Marin groaned. "I swear that man never sleeps. You'd think having a lover and a baby on the way would mellow him a bit." Her gaze met Ash's. "The general wants me to update him in person. I need to meet him in the Command Center. Now."

Ash mentally cursed. It looked like his night of luring Marin into his bed wasn't happening this evening. "I'll head off."

"Right." She fidgeted with her hair again.

He reached out and grabbed some of her curls. "I want to have that drink with you, Marin."

"A date?"

"I don't date. But I want to get you tipsy and kiss you again." His voice lowered. "And more."

She licked her lips. "Okay," she breathed.

"I also want to watch you touch yourself and not just imagine it in my head."

The air whistled between her teeth. "Ash."

He lowered his head, his lips brushing hers. "And I want to taste you again. Lick and suck you again until you explode."

Marin's belly contracted, her hands flexing on his arms. "Ash."

He tucked her curls back behind her ear. "That's exactly how I want you to say my name when you come. Later, Princess."

"Bye."

"Sweet dreams."

CHAPTER SEVEN

A sh heard a chime ringing through his dream. His dream of Marin. A very naked Marin with her curls falling around creamy shoulders.

"Ash. Rise and shine. We're on call."

Indy's voice burst the last image of his dream and he sat up in his bed. His room was pitch black. He touched the comms unit. "I'm up."

"Squad Three just got called in."

He swung out of bed, slapped the lights on, and grabbed some clothes off the floor. "What's happened?"

"Two techs went out at dawn to look at some malfunctioning cameras on the northern end of the Enclave. A raptor patrol came out of nowhere."

Shit. "Any soldiers with them?"

"Yeah," Indy said. "Mac and Taylor from Squad Nine."

Two damn good soldiers. Ash knew from firsthand

experience that those two stomped on any old-school argument that women didn't belong on the front line.

"But they're pinned down a distance from the techs. And one of the techs managed to get himself nabbed by a raptor."

Ash yanked on his shirt and then a nasty thought occurred to him. He paused. No, Marin had been up late. She wouldn't be out at dawn.

"Who got nabbed?" he asked.

"A guy called Eric. The other tech is Marin. Blonde with curls."

Ash closed his eyes for a second, then strode to his weapons locker. *Fuck.* He grabbed a carbine. "On my way."

He slammed out of his room, trying to tamp down the hot lick of panic in his gut. A few doors down, he saw Levi step into the corridor.

His best friend lifted his chin. "Hey. Got the call that two geeks tangled with some raptors."

Ash strode past, and caught a glimpse of a naked brunette sprawled bonelessly in Levi's bed before the door closed.

"We've gotta move," Ash said, breaking into a jog.

"What? Wait."

But Ash didn't wait. Marin needed him. He ran through the tunnels with Levi following. When they reached the northernmost entrance, he saw Tane and the rest of the squad waiting for them.

Ash slowed. "How'd the raptors get so close to the Enclave?" Anger was hitting him now. Marin should never have stepped outside if it wasn't safe.

Tane raised a brow. "Morning. The drones didn't see the aliens because they popped out of the ground. Looks like they used some existing tunnels from a neighboring coal mine. And the cameras in the area were malfunctioning."

"Let's go get our people," Ash said.

Tane opened the door and Ash was the first to push out into the morning sunlight.

"Where's the fire, Ash?" Griff grumbled from behind him.

Ash scanned the field of green grass, dotted with stands of trees. It was all drenched with bright morning light.

Indy gave them directions, and the squad moved together. Ash's jaw was tight, his hands clenched on his weapon. *Fucking be okay, Marin.*

Suddenly, a burst of carbine fire sounded ahead of them. Ash broke into a sprint.

"Ash!" Tane bit out.

But Ash had one driving need. Get to Marin.

He rounded a group of trees. He instantly spotted Mac and Taylor up on a hill. They were hunkered down behind some rocks, firing on the raptors down below.

A tall, lanky blond man was being dragged by a raptor by the collar of his shirt. Terror was etched on the man's features. The raptor was heading toward another pair who were returning fire with Mac and Taylor.

Where was Marin? Ash scanned around, his heart thumping hard. Then he spotted her, pinned down behind a tree, not far from the raptors. Her gaze was locked on her tech team colleague, concern on her face.

"Squad Three, six more raptors have appeared to the west of you." Indy's urgent voice on the comms.

"Damn." Tane lifted his head. "Levi, Ash, get the techs out. Rest of you, you're with me."

The others broke off, and Ash and Levi started down the slope. Eric was struggling weakly and the raptor lifted a huge fist and punched the man in the face. Eric cried out, blood streaming from his nose.

"Let's make some noise, brother," Levi said, lifting his carbine.

Ash nodded and together, they strode out of cover, firing.

Two raptors swiveled to fire at them. Levi ducked and rolled, coming up on his belly to fire at the aliens. Mac and Taylor continued giving them cover fire. Ash ducked into the trees and raced up to Marin.

"Ash!"

He gripped her arms, scanning her. "You okay?"

She nodded, one of her hands pressing to his chest. "Eric. We have to help him."

"I'm taking you back inside."

Her fingers twisted. "No! He doesn't have that long. Please. He's kind, and smart, and naïve. Please, help him."

Shit. He couldn't damn well say no to her. "I'll get him. You stay here and stay down."

Ash spun and used the trees to duck and weave closer to the whimpering man and his captor.

One of the raptors was down, but the other was still firing. Eric's captor was still dragging him away.

Trusting Levi to have his back, Ash strode out and fired.

Surprised, the alien dropped Eric and dived. Ash strode up to him and kicked him. The raptor tried to swing his weapon around, but Ash was already firing. When the alien stopped moving, Ash turned to the downed tech.

"Eric!" Marin barreled in.

Dammit. Ash threw an arm out and she ran into it. "I told you to stay in cover."

"He needs help."

Mac and Taylor fired again. Ash grabbed Marin and turned. Beyond the trees, he saw two new raptors appear out of nowhere. There must be another tunnel nearby.

"Marin, I need to you to get back in cover behind a tree."

She saw the raptors, her eyes widening. Ash yanked out his laser pistol and thrust it into her hand.

"Do you know how to fire this?"

"No."

Shit. "It's just a precaution. Only use it if you have to. It's like in the game. Safety off, point, and shoot. Aim for the chest."

She nodded, her face pale, but she was holding it together. He yanked her close and pressed a fast kiss to her lips.

"Stay down and stay safe."

She nodded and Ash spun away. He lifted his carbine and headed for the new raptors. They were closing in on Eric.

Ash fired and took one down. He swung to the other and pulled the trigger. His carbine jammed. *Fuck.*

The raptor made a sound like a laugh, bringing his big, scaled weapon up.

Ash yanked out his combat knife, knowing he wasn't going to be fast enough. Laser fire sprayed the ground near the raptor. The alien jerked. Ash turned his head and saw Marin advancing, holding the pistol in a perfect two-handed grip.

Fear and anger rushed into his chest. *Damn her.* He wondered how the hell he could be equal parts mad and proud. He turned, lifted his hand, and threw his knife. It hit the raptor's throat, blood spraying. The alien staggered back, gurgling, then collapsed.

Marin ran forward. "Eric!"

"Oh, God, Marin," the man said, voice shaky.

Ash pressed his lips into a hard line and grabbed her arm. "What the fuck did you think you were doing?"

"Helping you."

"This isn't fucking Pre-Emptive Strike, Marin." He saw Taylor and Mac headed toward them, and the rest of his squad heading over. Eric was sitting up, holding his bleeding nose.

Ash didn't care. All he saw was Marin walking toward a goddamned raptor.

"I ordered you to stay back in cover."

Marin drew herself up, her eyes narrowing. "Last time I checked, I didn't take orders from you."

"Out here you do."

"No. See, I have this thing—" she waved a hand at her

head "—it's called a brain. I use it to think and make my own damn decisions." She stomped past him.

Damn. So his sweet geek had some spit and fire. He liked it.

Ash grabbed her shoulder and spun her around. She gasped, and he pulled her up, sank a hand in her hair, and took her mouth with his.

He slid his tongue between her lips, drinking her in. Heat rocketed through him, mixing with all the volatile emotions churning inside him. When she moaned and kissed him back, savage satisfaction hit him.

When he dropped her back on her feet, she had a dazed look on her face.

"She's yours?" Levi stared at them, brows raised.

Ash pulled back, but kept her close. "Yes."

"No." Marin yanked away from him, her eyes clearing.

Levi grinned, and from behind him, Hemi let out a laugh.

She glared at Ash, then turned and stomped over to Eric.

Tane shook his head, looking down at the ground. "This should be interesting."

ASH JOINED his squad for breakfast at a table in the dining room. They'd all showered and cleaned up after their little morning expedition. Most of the Enclave had eaten and headed off for the day, so they had the place to themselves.

There was no sign of Marin. He figured she was locked in the tech lab or sitting by Eric's side in the infirmary. Ash decided it was better to let her cool off a bit.

He grinned. Just a bit.

"So, you and the curly-haired cutie from the tech team?" Levi leaned back in his chair.

Ash set his plate down and sat. "Yep."

Hemi snorted. "From where I was standing, it looked like you'd blown it."

Ash chewed on some toast. "She'll come around." He shook his head. "Don't know how the hell you deal with Cam going out in the field every day."

The big man shrugged. "She's trained and she's badass. If I told her not to go, she'd kick my ass."

Ash nodded. Marin didn't belong in the field, or anywhere near fucking raptors.

"Hey." Indy appeared. "I lost the damn comms for the last part of the rescue. The tech team are fixing the problem. What did I miss?"

The men all grinned.

"Nothing," Ash said.

Indy's eyes narrowed. "I can tell you're all lying."

"We saved the day," Hemi said. "Rescued the girl. Well, the guy. The girl was too busy being kick ass."

Indy's brows rose. "Really? Well, the girl, who is actually a super smart woman has an update on her spider bot. The general wants you down in the Command Center in—" Indy looked at her watch "—three minutes ago."

There were grumbles and groans. Ash drained his juice and stood. They all headed for the Command

Center and when they entered, he saw a group gathered for the briefing.

Holmes looked over. "Nice of you to join us."

Ash spotted Marin straight away, standing beside Noah. Her wild curls were pulled up in a mess on her head, and she had a pen stuck in there.

She glanced his way and shot him a glare. His damn cock twitched, and he winked at her.

"Listen up, everyone," Holmes said. "Marin has an update for us."

Marin cleared her throat and looked around the room. "The spider bot connected with the alien system and is transmitting."

Holmes nodded. "Which is great news."

Tane crossed his arms over his chest. "But?"

"But it can't break all the encryptions," Marin said. "I've tried several algorithms—"

"Don't talk geek," Tane said.

She nodded. "The line is live, but nothing can get through."

There were murmurs around the room, and Holmes looked pensive.

"We might be able to break through in time," Noah ground out. "But it'll likely take months. Unsurprisingly, the Gizzida have their central hub well-protected."

"We might not be here in months," Griff murmured.

"I think I can break the encryption faster," Marin said.

Ash stiffened. He heard something buried in her voice.

"How much faster?" Holmes asked.

"In minutes."

"But there's a catch, isn't there?" Ash said.

Her gaze whipped up to his. "Well..."

He saw the muscle beside her mouth twitch and his gut tightened.

She shifted her feet. "I need to be on site to do it."

"What?" Ash's exclamation was joined by Noah's.

"If I can be close to the data hub and my spider bot, I know I can break through the raptor security and access their information."

Ash surged forward, but Tane grabbed his arm. Noah turned, a fierce scowl on his face.

Holmes held up a hand. "Marin, can we hook you up with comms? You can talk a squad through the steps from here."

She shook her head. "The hub is likely going to be deep in the tunnel complex, and comms aren't guaranteed."

"How can the bot transmit data, then?" Levi asked.

"It's hooked into the alien system, and will use that to amplify the signal and get data to our nearest drone."

Holmes stroked his jaw. "Can you give a squad instructions and they can do the job on site?"

Marin shook her head. "The instructions are far too complex—"

"We aren't dumb grunts," Ash bit out.

She lifted her chin. "I never said that. But I've been studying this all my life, and some of it I won't even know until I'm there. I can't give you a five-minute lesson."

She wanted him to take her into the heart of raptor territory. Into danger. Ash felt like his head was going to explode. "You already tangled with a raptor." He couldn't handle her being surrounded by them. "Noah can go."

Marin stepped forward. "Not even he can do what I can. And just because he's a man means he gets to risk his life to help, but I can't?"

"It's not that."

She crossed her arms over her chest, a stubborn look settling over her features.

He turned to look at Holmes and Tane. "You can't be seriously considering allowing this. She is not made to be in the field."

"We need the data." A resigned look settled on the general's face.

"Fuck!" Ash saw Marin flinch.

"I understand your reluctance to take Marin into the field," Holmes said, his voice lowering. "I've been forced to make many hard decisions in order to ensure our survival. Including taking my own woman into alien territory. We had raptors come out of the ground right on our doorstep. We need every advantage when it comes to keeping the Enclave and our people safe." He paused. "Marin will have protection."

She sure as hell would. Him. Ash glared at her and she glared back. If she was going into this hub, he'd be at her side every step of the damn way.

"Twenty-four hours," Holmes said. "Plan the mission, minimize the chance of any contact with the Gizzida. Get in, let Marin do what she needs to do, and then get out."

Just the thought of the raptors being anywhere near her, the thought she might actually get hurt, sent wild anger churning through Ash. He had a pretty long fuse, but when he lost it, he lost it. He needed to cool off.

He spun and stalked out. He needed a drink or, better yet, he needed to hit something.

CHAPTER EIGHT

A sh had been so angry.

A few hours after Ash had stormed out of the meeting, Marin stopped in the corridor and pressed her back to the wall.

Clearly, he didn't think she could do it. He thought she was fierce in a stupid computer game, but not in real life. He'd proven that when she'd tried to help him during the raptor attack outside. He'd turned into a damn brainless caveman.

She was sexy and interesting, as long as she was safely tucked up in the tech lab.

A part of her was scared. She didn't want to go into the middle of alien territory and possibly face down raptors. But she'd do it.

Some kids ran past her, laughing. They were a reminder of why she'd do it. She'd do her part to fight back against the aliens, and fight for humanity's right to survive.

Pushing away from the wall, she continued down the corridor. All her life, she'd been good at hiding. She'd perfected the art of being invisible. Her mother had wanted her to be the perfect socialite, while her father had been too absorbed in his work to care what Marin did. Her mother had made it an artform to pick on Marin's looks, her lack of social graces, the time she spent studying.

Instead of standing up to them, Marin had withdrawn and buried herself in her studies.

"Marin."

Ash's voice made her stiffen. This time, instead of running, she turned to face him.

"Do you know what it's like out there?" he snapped.

She sighed. "Yes."

"You have no idea." He pushed her until her back bumped into the wall. He moved in close, big and overpowering. The spicy scent of him surrounded her.

"I think—"

"The raptors are bigger, stronger, crueler." His tone was biting. "And you want me to take you deep into the heart of a fucking facility crawling with them."

She swallowed. "I know. But I'll have protection."

"This isn't a game, Marin. It's not Pre-Emptive Strike out there. That was real raptor fire out there this morning!"

"I know that, Ash. I'm not stupid, and I'm not helpless."

He growled, and then pushed away from her. He paced the corridor and jammed a hand through his hair. "I know you aren't stupid. But it still scares the shit out of me." He looked back at her, his jaw tight. "I don't want you to get hurt."

Something in her chest opened and bloomed. It had been a really long time since someone had cared about protecting her. Noah was a great boss and looked out for everyone on the team. But she knew, in the dark of night, there was no one on the planet thinking of her.

Ash spun away, pressing his hands to the wall. She saw the tense muscles in his back under his shirt. She tried to hold on to her anger from the morning, but it slipped away. She moved closer to him, her pulse racing, and pressed a hand to the middle of his back. Those hard muscles flexed under her palm.

"Your squad will be with me. You'll be with me. I trust you to protect me, SuperSoldier."

He spun and yanked her close. "I will. With my life."

Marin's heart knocked against her chest. "I'd prefer that you didn't get hurt or killed."

"There are no guarantees out there, Princess."

God. The thought of Ash getting hurt made her knees weak.

"I'll be right beside you on the mission. I won't fucking let a raptor near you."

"I know."

They stared at each other.

"Too fucking trusting, Marin."

Ash moved and Marin leaped at him. He caught her, hauling her up, and she wrapped her legs around his waist.

"You're mine," he growled. "Tonight, you're mine, Marin."

"Yes." She pressed her lips to his jaw. She'd faced down a raptor today, and in twenty-four hours, she was heading into an alien base, so she was going to keep up her brave streak.

She was going to find out what being with Ash Connors felt like.

He strode down the corridor and they both ignored the startled looks of the people they passed. Before she knew it, he was letting them into his quarters.

Ash turned on lights, his lips landing on hers. *Yes.*

Marin slid her hands into his hair and kissed him back.

MARIN WENT wild in Ash's arms. He loved how greedy she was, how she forgot herself and lost herself in the pleasure. She pressed into him, kissing him back frantically. He felt her fingers digging into his scalp, and he wrapped his arms around her curvy body and pulled her closer. He wanted nothing between them.

He carried her over to the bed and laid her on it. A few quick tugs and he stripped her clothes off her.

She automatically moved to cover herself.

"No, don't." He grabbed her wrist. "You're gorgeous."

"I'm not slim and elegant."

"Who cares about slim and fucking elegant? I'm a biker. I like tits and ass."

She blushed. "Really?"

He remembered the things she'd confessed to him while they'd been gaming. Her mother, and a bunch of ruthless kids at school, had really done a number on her. His gaze skated over her full breasts. They were covered in a blush of pink, with nipples tightened to hard points.

"Look at these pretty tits." He cupped them, then leaned down and sucked one pink nipple into his mouth. She cried out.

He sucked, then swirled his tongue, before raising his head. He ran his hands down the curve of her belly.

"Soft and cute."

"Soft bellies are not—"

"Are just how I like a woman." He pressed open-mouthed kisses to the sweet curve of her belly. She arched up into him.

Then he turned her on her side, sliding his hands over her to caress her ass. Oh yeah, he liked her ass, a lot. He gave one cheek a little slap. She gasped.

"Every time I look at this sweet ass, I get hard."

She made a husky sound, and Ash leaned down and gently bit one cheek. Then he sat back, pushing her onto her belly.

"Ash?"

"Trust me, Princess. I'm going to take good care of you." He slid a hand between her thighs.

She cried out, lifting her ass up, which gave him better access.

She was already wet and he stroked her. Damn, she was gorgeous. "I need another taste of you."

"I heard you love to...uh, go down on women."

He paused. "Did you?"

She looked back over her shoulder, and couldn't possibly know just how sexy she looked.

He slid two fingers inside her, loving her moan, and the way she rocked her hips against his hand. "Whoever told you that isn't right."

"Oh?" Her voice was husky.

"Nope. I'm equal opportunity. I love having my cock sucked, too."

He flicked at her clit, and her cry was sharp. He slid to his knees beside the bed, pressing a quick kiss to the base of her spine, right above her sweet buttocks. Then he didn't give her any time to prepare, just circled her thighs with his hands, nudged them apart, and closed his mouth on her.

As he delved his tongue deep, he heard her ragged breaths. Her thigh muscles tensed, but she pushed back against him.

"Ash...too much."

He brushed her swollen clit with his tongue. "Not enough, sweetheart. Damn, you taste like heaven. Don't hold back."

"I need..." Her hands twisted in the covers.

"What, Princess? This?" He sucked on her clit.

She shattered. Her whole body froze for a second, then she was convulsing, his name a husky cry on her lips.

Ash stood, tearing his clothes off.

Marin pushed up on her elbows and rolled over. She watched him hungrily. He could see she was excited, watching each piece of him that he uncovered. Her gaze traced over his chest, his tattoos, and down his belly. He quickly undid his jeans and shoved them off.

Her eyes widened. "Holy..."

"Like what you see?" he asked with a smile.

"You're...big."

She reared up on her knees and reached out. She stroked her fingers down his arms, tracing his ink. Then she released a shaky breath and stared at his cock.

"I want your cock in my mouth." She blinked, looking surprised. "Um, did I just say that aloud?"

He smiled and took a step closer to the bed. "Sure did."

He pushed her down on the covers, loving seeing her curls spread out on the sheets. He leaned over her. "You want your pretty lips on my cock, Princess?"

"Yes." Her eyes were heated.

He circled the base of his cock, hoping that he could hold it together, and give her what she wanted. Love her the way she deserved.

Pre-come beaded on the head of his cock and her eyes were glued to it. She licked her lips and he groaned. He brushed the tip of his cock over her lips, coating them. Her tongue darted out, flicking over the tip of him. He groaned again.

Then she opened her mouth and sucked him in.

Fuck.

MARIN WAS JUST ADJUSTING to having Ash's large cock in her mouth, loving the musky taste of him, when he pulled back.

She made a cry of protest and looked up. His handsome face was set in stark lines.

"First time I come with you, it won't be in your mouth, Marin." His hands gripped her thighs, pushing them apart. He climbed onto the bed, his big body covering hers. "First time I come, it'll be deep inside you."

Yes. "I have a contraceptive implant."

"Me, too. One of doc's new ones."

Marin felt the hard prod of his cock between her legs. She shivered and their gazes locked.

"Sweet, fierce Marin," he murmured. Then he pushed inside her.

God, the stretch. He was big, and she hadn't had sex in a long time. She pushed her head back into the bed. As the hard inches of him slid inside her, she felt consumed.

"So damn tight." His voice was a growl. "You want this, Princess?"

"Yes."

"Good. You'll take it all."

He pulled out and then slammed back in. Marin cried out, her hands digging into his shoulders.

"Perfect," he growled. "I knew it would be."

"Ash."

He kept thrusting inside her, reaching down to readjust the angle of her hips. On the next thrust, he hit some sensitive spot inside her. *Oh, Jesus.*

His hips kept working at a fast pace, and she looked past him and caught a glimpse of them in the mirror. She watched his tight ass working between her splayed legs. Her belly spasmed. It was so sexy to watch him taking her. His tattooed arms held him propped up, the muscles in his ass flexing.

"Are you ready, Marin?"

"For...what?"

"To come. Hard."

His thrusts increased, the bedframe slamming against the wall. Her gaze dropped down, and she watched the ripple of his abs as he thrust inside her.

"Eyes here, Marin."

She met his gaze. They looked more blue, dark and intense. He thrust deeper, reaching some place inside her that had every sensation within her exploding. Her orgasm crashed over her, the pleasure coming in waves. She screamed and didn't care that it was probably loud enough for the entire base to hear.

Ash thrust inside her one last time, his body jerking. With a shout, he poured himself inside her.

Marin stared into his handsome face. She could spend hours just looking at him. She'd finally just had amazing, once-in-a-lifetime sex with the sexiest man in the world.

She, Marin Mitchell, had snagged a hot bad boy. She giggled.

Ash pulled out of her, his gaze curious. "Should I be worried that you're laughing right now?"

She shook her head. "No. It was perfect. Amazing. But I'm pretty sure we tore a hole in the fabric of space-time."

"What?"

"Hot badass berserkers do not have sex with geeky tech girls."

He sent her a sexy smile. "Well, this berserker does, with my sexy, hot geeky tech girl. Now—" he tugged her close, giving her butt a light slap. "Time to get some rest."

"Rest?" she said, breathing in the scent of him. It felt so nice to be wrapped up in his strength.

"You need some rest because I want to fuck you again soon."

Oh. Oh. "I don't really think I need a rest."

CHAPTER NINE

"So damn tight," Ash ground out.

He had Marin's knees pushed to her chest and was pounding into her. She was making small, husky cries as he thrust deep, her hands twisting in the sheets.

He didn't slow his pace and kept his gaze glued to her face. He wanted to watch when he tipped her over the edge.

"Ash!"

"Let it come, sweetheart. Squeeze down on my cock and come." He reached a hand between her legs and pressed on her clit.

Her body went tense, and then she screamed so loud he was sure his neighbors heard. Ash didn't give a fuck. As her body clamped down on his cock, he kept thrusting, his own explosion imminent. Sweat dripped off his face as he watched her ride out her orgasm.

Another two thrusts and his release hit. He lodged deep and poured himself inside her.

Ash stroked a hand down her side before he slid out from inside her. He helped her lower her legs and then collapsed on the bed beside her. He curled around her and pulled her close.

She let out a satisfied sigh. "That's a pretty good way to wake up."

"Fuck yeah." He breathed in the scent of her hair. He'd spent most of the night inside her. Whenever he'd woken, he'd roll over, hungry for her again. And she'd been the same, lighting up, as hungry as he was. Then he remembered what they were doing today.

Tonight, he had to take her to the alien hub.

When he stiffened, she went still. "Um...is something wrong?"

"There's nothing wrong when I have you naked in my arms." He sighed. "Just thinking of the mission."

She turned to face him. "I can do this, Ash."

"I have no doubt you can. Doesn't mean I'm not scared shitless about taking you out there."

She bit down on her lip.

He sank a hand into her curls. "You're mine now, Marin. I've claimed you."

"Is that a biker thing?"

"No, it's an Ash thing. I've seen your pretty tits, sucked on your clit, heard you cry out my name in that sexy, husky voice of yours, seen your cute toes."

She let out a startled laugh. "My toes?"

"Yep. All mine."

She touched her lips to his. "I guess that means you're mine, too."

"Hell yeah, Princess." His smile slipped away. "I

don't want you to get hurt. Hated seeing anyone hurt, ever since I was a kid. That's why I always wanted to become a doctor."

"You would have been a great doctor. You have the kind of face people trust. Not sure I can see you in a lab coat, though."

"Tats might scare some people off."

She ran a finger over his cheek. "Have you ever wanted to go back to it?"

"Medicine?" He shook his head. "I'm a soldier, Marin. A fighter."

She frowned. "Or is that just the box you've put yourself in? I put myself in a few boxes when I was younger." A rueful smile. "I still do now."

He rolled her over and nipped her lips. "Well, you are firmly in the berserker babe box now."

She laughed. "That is one box I would never have put myself in." Her voice lowered. "But I like it."

"Good. Now, we need to get you prepped for the mission," he continued. "You need armor and a weapon."

She pushed at her hair, trying to sort out the tangled curls. "Okay."

"We have the day to do it, and then we head out on the mission tonight."

She lifted her chin. "I'll be ready."

"Come on." He held out a hand and pulled her off the bed.

Ash kept their shower quick...mostly. They dressed and he tugged her out into the hall, keeping a tight hold on her hand.

He'd never been the hand-holding type. Mostly

because his hookups had never lasted long, and the few women he'd been with longer than a couple of nights weren't the hand-holding types, either. He laced his fingers with Marin's, realizing he liked holding her hand.

"Where are we going?" she asked.

"I'm going to ask a friend to help get you prepped."

"Who?"

"Claudia. From Hell Squad."

Marin jerked to a halt. "Claudia? She is *ah-mazing*. She's my dream woman." Marin's blue eyes came alive. "I want to be her when I grow up."

The babbling made him smile. "You're cute."

Her nose wrinkled. "Women don't want to be cute, Ash. They want to be strong and sexy."

"Marin, you're cute. Own it." He leaned closer and lowered his voice. "Cute works for me. A lot."

Her gaze turned considering, moving over his face. "One day, you'll wake up and cute won't be enough."

"You're wrong." He tugged her down the corridor. With Marin, he realized now that he had to prove things to her logical mind. Arguing with her was pointless.

They traveled through a couple more hallways, and then he knocked on a door.

Marin fidgeted. "If I go all speechless fangirl, slap me or something."

"Cute," he muttered.

The door opened, and a lanky, shaggy-haired man leaned in the doorway.

"Hey, Ash." Shaw's gaze dropped to Ash and Marin's linked hands, his eyes widening. When he looked back up, he smiled. "You bringing me a pretty woman? I like the idea, but I already have one, and she might not be so happy about it."

"Shaw. You know Marin."

"From the tech team. How are you, Marin?" Hell Squad's sniper asked.

She cleared her throat. "Fine, thanks."

"Marin's coming with us on the data hub mission. She needs armor and a weapon—"

Claudia appeared, elbowing Shaw out of the way. "Hi, Ash."

"Hey, Claudia. I was hoping you could help get Marin prepped for a mission."

"Hi, Marin," Claudia said.

Marin was staring at Claudia with big eyes filled with awe. She managed a nod.

Ash kept his gaze direct on Claudia's face, communicating how important this was to him. The female soldier's dark eyes glinted and she nodded.

"Don't worry, Connors. I'll take care of your girl."

Marin startled. "Oh, I'm not—"

Ash turned, pulled Marin up on her toes, and kissed her. When he was done, he released her, satisfied to see her eyes were glazed.

"I'll see you later," he told her. He nodded at the couple. "Thanks, Claudia."

As he strode down the hall, he heard Shaw chuckle. "Never argue with a berserker, Marin."

MARIN FOUND herself following Claudia into the

Enclave's firing range, trying to keep up with the woman's long strides. The tough woman moved with an easy, athletic gait, her long, dark braid swinging behind her.

"The thermo pistol will be the best weapon for you," Claudia said. "It's small and easy to use. When the bullets hit, they heat up. Raptors don't like them, and the creepers *really* hate them."

Marin had only ever fired a weapon once in her life. And that had been yesterday morning.

"You just need to point and shoot," Claudia added.

"Point and shoot. Right." Marin glanced around the range. Several lanes were set up with targets at the end.

One woman was using the far lane, holding a carbine up, her intense focus on the targets. Captain Kate Scott, head of Enclave security, held the weapon like she knew exactly what to do with it. Her dark hair fell just shy of her shoulders, and she had an unsmiling face.

"Don't worry, Curls," Claudia said. "We'll practice a little, and then we need to get upstairs and find you some armor that'll fit." The soldier's gaze drifted down Marin's form.

Curls. Marin fought back wrinkling her nose. Of course she'd end up with a cute nickname.

"Frost? What brings you here?" a deep voice said.

Marin spun and saw a huge man standing nearby. He was dressed in black-and-gray fatigue trousers, with a black T-shirt molded over a huge chest. His massive arms were crossed, and a hint of black ink peeked out from under one sleeve. His face had strong features that showed his Maori heritage clearly, and it was obvious that he was related to Tane and Hemi.

"Hi, Manu. I have a newbie who needs to borrow a thermo pistol. Your brothers are taking her out on a mission."

Manu's dark gaze flicked to Marin, and she had to brace herself not to take a step back.

"Always knew they were crazy," Manu said. "What's a small thing like you want to go into raptor chaos for?"

"Well, I'm a tech genius, and only I can hack into the aliens' data hub."

Manu stared at her for a second, before a small smile appeared on his face. "Then we'd better get you a thermo pistol." His gaze moved over to the occupied lane. "If the captain follows her usual routine, and she always does—" his tone was dry "—then she's almost finished, so you'll have the place to yourself. Pick a lane, and don't forget your hearing protection."

Before long, Marin found herself with sleek earmuffs on her head, holding a small gun, and firing again and again on Claudia's orders. The woman was a hard taskmaster, correcting Marin's grip and stance, and making her practice over and over.

Finally, Claudia nodded and slipped her earmuffs down around her neck. "You'll do."

Relieved, Marin set the pistol on the bench. Her arms were burning from holding them up. She really needed to get to the gym more, and she wondered if Ash would take her.

Ash. Her thoughts instantly went to what they'd done to each other, all night long. She'd had more orgasms in the last few days than she'd had in her entire life. She clenched her thighs. She could still feel his touch, and taste his kiss—

"Earth to Curls."

Claudia's amused voice made Marin blink and focus on the other woman.

"You need to concentrate on the upcoming mission," Claudia said. "Distractions will get you killed."

"Killed. Right. That would be bad." Marin swallowed. "Sorry, I—"

Claudia grinned. "Mission, not sexy-as-hell berserkers."

Marin blushed. Damn, her pale skin. "Um..."

"Time for armor." Claudia pocketed the thermo pistol, and lifted a hand to wave goodbye to Manu.

The pair of them headed through the corridors. They reached the squad locker rooms and Claudia led her into Hell Squad's. "I think I have some old armor that Elle wore. That should fit you."

"Elle goes in the field?"

"She's been a couple of times. She tangled with a rex once." Claudia grinned. "Marcus almost lost his shit over that."

Marin could imagine that hard, tough Marcus Steele wouldn't like his wife tangling with a giant tyrannosaurus rex-like alien.

Claudia opened a locker and started pulling out some pieces of armor, eyeing Marin up and down with each new item. Some pieces she laid out on a nearby bench, some she shoved away.

The door swung open. "Howdy, chickies."

Indy strode in, cradling a huge travel mug of what

smelled like coffee. The scent hit Marin and made her tied-in-knots stomach turn over.

Her gaze was drawn to the gorgeous rose-and-thorn tattoos down the woman's arms. The blood-red color of the ink looked striking with Indy's bronze skin and black hair. She was wearing a tank top, and as she turned to settle on a bench, Marin caught a glimpse of a large cross tattooed on her back. Marin gave a mental sigh. The woman was so attractive.

"Curls?"

Marin blinked. "Sorry, sorry. I am paying attention. I'm just nervous."

"You're thinking about your sexy guy again," Claudia teased.

"No." But as soon as she thought of Ash, memories intruded. She shivered, feeling the ache between her thighs.

Indy sat up. "You seeing someone on the tech team?"

"No." Marin hoped her voice didn't sound high-pitched. Claudia was smirking.

"Civilian?"

"Ah, no."

"So it's a squad member, then?" Indy leaned forward and sipped her coffee. "You have a thing for a soldier?"

Marin shifted nervously. "Maybe. But I...I'm not like you two."

Claudia's brows rose. "What do you mean?"

"Confident, attractive, bold."

"You're cute and smart," Claudia said. "Believe me, a big, tough guy would trip over himself to wrap you up and keep you all to himself."

Marin chewed on her lip. "Really?"

Indy nodded. "All those curls, that cute, curvy body you keep hidden, and the intelligence that shines off you. They'd want to be all over that."

"No tough guy ever has before."

"And just how many tough guys were you in proximity to before the invasion?" Indy sipped her coffee, one eyebrow raised.

Marin tilted her head. "Well...technically, none. My dad was a professor at a university, and my mother was the ideal society wife. Always having perfect dinner parties, and hoping I'd morph into her vision of a perfect daughter." Marin heard the bitterness and hurt in her own voice. "And of course, date and marry the perfect guy."

Indy nodded. "The alien invasion has pushed so many different people together. Young and old, rich and poor, soldier and geek." Then a frown appeared on the woman's face. "Shame it still hasn't opened some stubborn people's eyes."

"Just be yourself," Claudia said. "Don't let him boss you around."

Indy nodded. "If he doesn't like you as you are, fuck him. Life's too short for that shit." There was venom in her voice. Marin wondered who the unlucky guy was who'd pissed her off.

"He seems to like me. A lot."

"And Ash Connors strikes me as a man who knows exactly what he likes." Claudia winked.

Indy spluttered her coffee. "Ash? You're sleeping with Ash?" The woman grinned. "Oh, my God, you are so perfect for him. He's so smart but tries to downplay it." Her eyes narrowed. "Wait...the incident outside the Enclave. He told the guys he's into you, didn't he? They all knew but they didn't tell me." Her mouth twisted. "Bastards."

"Ignore her." Claudia held up some armor and started strapping it onto Marin. "Here we go. Arms out."

Marin obeyed, watching as the woman circled her, clipping things up, adjusting bits here and there.

"There. Done." Claudia stepped back.

Marin turned and looked in the mirror on the wall. God, she looked like a soldier. *Hello, PrincessBadass.* Well, she looked like a soldier with wild, curly blonde hair. "Thanks, Claudia."

"Let me show you how the controls for the armor illusion system work." She pointed to a panel on the side of the armor.

"I worked on the project for the armor illusion system."

"Good. And now you'll get to see it working up close and personal in the field."

The nerves came back full-force. "Oh, God."

"You'll be fine, honey," Indy said. "You'll have six big, over-protective berserkers sticking to you like glue."

"Oh, God."

"Here's your thermo pistol." Claudia helped her holster it and stow the extra ammunition. The Hell Squad soldier crossed her arms over her chest and nodded. "Looking good. You'll also need some cedar oil grenades."

Fear, dark and insidious, started creeping into Marin's system. She tried to force it back. Cedar oil grenades were for repelling canids. Huge, slavering alien hunting dogs, with spikes and sharp teeth. When Marin was little, a neighbor's dog had attacked her. Her father had chased it off with a bat, but she'd been afraid of dogs ever since.

Maybe Ash was right. She shouldn't be going on this mission.

Marin let Claudia tuck the grenades into slots on her belt. She didn't want to go out there, and she was well aware of how dangerous it was.

But she *had* to go.

She had to do this job, for everyone at the Enclave, for herself, for all the squad soldiers like Ash who went out there and fought every day. She had to do this to give humanity a fighting chance.

"How do you make the fear go away?" she asked Claudia.

The woman paused. "You don't. It never goes away, and if it does, you're fucked. You need it. You use it. Ride it, and let it make you more determined and more careful."

The locker room door opened, and a wolf whistle pierced the air. Marin's head jerked up, and she watched Shaw enter.

"Nothing like a group of sexy, tough women to make a man's mouth water," the sniper drawled.

"There should be only one sexy, tough woman you care about," Indy said from the bench.

"I'm allowed to look, just not touch." Shaw snagged

an arm around Claudia and pulled her in for a hard, thorough kiss.

Claudia sank her hands into Shaw's tawny hair and kissed him back.

Something in Marin sighed. They looked so good together. A perfect fit.

Shaw lifted his head. "Looking good, Curls. My woman did a bloody good job."

Marin smiled nervously and held her arms out. "I almost look like my character in Pre-Emptive Strike." Her smile faded. "But I know it's nothing like a game out there."

Indy stood and moved closer to grip Marin's arm. "I'll be in your ear. And my guys, they might be rough and tough, but they'll take good care of you."

She nodded. "Thanks." This was it. The real deal.

"Good luck out there, Marin," Claudia said.

"Thank you. For everything."

"Go kick some raptor ass," Claudia said with a wink.

Marin walked with Indy toward the Hawk hangar. They made a stop at the tech lab, so Marin could grab her field kit and get a stern pep talk from Noah. She could see he was worried and that made her nerves worse.

As they entered the hangar, Marin barely paid any attention to the quadcopters. Her gaze zeroed in on the tough group of men waiting by the closest Hawk. They were laughing and joking, all of them ruggedly attractive in different ways. She looked at Ash and his head lifted, like he'd sensed her. He shot her a small smile.

"I need to get to the Command Center." Indy squeezed Marin's arm. "Good luck out there." She looked at the berserkers. "Hey, you bozos. Don't get yourselves killed out there."

As Indy left, Marin blew out a breath and marched toward Squad Three.

Tane looked her over and then gave a single nod. "Ready to go?"

"No," she answered honestly.

"You'll be fine." Ash was there, just inches from her.

His presence steadied her.

"We're taking two Hawks," Tane called out. "Our bikes are stored in the back of the quadcopters. Griff, Dom, and I will be in the first Hawk, the rest of you in the other. See you there."

Ash helped Marin climb into their Hawk. She sank onto one of the seats, trying not to fidget. Ash settled beside her, stretching out his long legs. Hemi and Levi came aboard, checking their weapons, and talking in low voices. They didn't sit, but stood instead, and held the handholds above their heads.

The engines started up, and the vibrations rippled through the aircraft. This was it. She, Marin Mitchell, self-professed geek, was heading out onto the battlefield.

"God, I'm going to be sick," she whispered.

A big hand touched the back of her neck and squeezed. "No, you're not."

She needed a distraction. She turned her head and her gaze fell on the three big bikes stored at the back of the Hawk. The vehicles were big, tough, and dangerous-looking. Perfect for berserkers.

The Hawk rose, flying upward through a vertical

tunnel of rock. They cleared the Enclave, swiveled, and headed north.

"Tell me the plan," she said, needing more of a distraction.

"We'll get dropped ten klicks from the tunnel entrance," Hemi said. "Don't want any scaly bastards to spot us. The bikes have illusion systems, and we'll go in... quietly." The big man snorted.

"We don't engage unless we have to," Ash said. "Fighting raptors will put Marin at risk. We get through the tunnels, get Marin to the hub, then get out."

Hemi lifted his chin.

"You'll be fine," Ash said to Marin. "You ride with me, and stay at my side the entire time."

She nodded, rubbing her hands over her thighs, listening to the low rumble of conversation around her. Ash was talking to Levi, but when he shifted, his big thigh brushed against hers. She hated that the armor separated them.

"If you get scared—" his voice lowered so only she could hear, his warm breath brushing her ear "—think of my mouth on you."

Her head jerked up. "Ash—"

"I'll be there with you, Marin. Whatever happens. I'll be your very own personal super soldier."

CHAPTER TEN

Ash felt the Hawk slowing, and knew they were nearing their drop-off point.

He didn't usually feel much fear. Hadn't, even as a kid. He'd grown up fearless. But with Marin beside him, he felt it now. *Lock it down, Connors.*

He sensed her tension, saw the fear she was trying to hide. He wouldn't make it any harder for her. Instead, he'd do what he was good at, and help her get this mission done.

The skids touched down and Hemi yanked the side door open. They'd landed in parkland, near a lake. It was overgrown and tangled, and he watched a flock of cockatoos rise up, squawking as they flew away. The sun was setting and soon they'd lose the light. The cover of darkness would help them sneak in.

Together, the three men lowered the ramp and rolled the bikes out. Ash turned back and saw Marin scanning their surroundings. In the distance, a street flanking the park was visible. Most of the houses were charred shells. He realized she wouldn't have been here in the ruins of the city before.

He reached over and gripped her waist. "Not pretty, is it?"

"It's horrible. Everything empty or destroyed." Her chest hitched. "So many people dead."

"You lost your parents?"

She nodded. "I was working here in Sydney, not too far from the Blue Mountains. I made it to Blue Mountain Base soon after the attack. I managed to call my parents in Chicago...I heard the raptors attack their house."

"I'm sorry, Marin." He remembered the chaos of the invasion. He and Levi, along with several Iron King members had fought back against the raptors, helped who they could. But eventually, it had only been him and Levi left, heading west on their bikes.

"Let's find this hub," Marin said fiercely. "For all the people we've lost."

When he led her to his bike, Levi and Hemi were already mounted on theirs. The second Hawk wasn't far away, and Ash could see Tane and the others unloading their bikes.

Soon, the Hawks lifted off, disappearing into a camouflaged shimmer in the darkening sky. Ash climbed onto his bike and started the silent engine. He patted the seat behind him. "Climb aboard."

He watched as her cheeks pinkened. Damn, so cute. What he didn't need right now was a hard-on.

"Lucky we have a dangerous mission ahead, or you'd

be making me think of you climbing aboard...other things."

She settled behind him. "Quit that. I need to focus."

Soon, the entire squad was mounted up.

"Time to ride," Tane said. "Illusion systems up."

"Hold on, Princess," Ash murmured.

She wrapped her arms around him and pressed her face against his back. Around them, his squad mates and their bikes blurred out of view. Ash flicked on his illusion system.

"Let's roll." Tane's voice came through Ash's earpiece.

"I've laid out the best route," Indy's voice sounded now. "If the drones pick anything else up, I'll let you know."

They took off out of the park and onto the road. Ash glanced at the screen attached to his bike controls, and kept an eye on the route. He slowly felt Marin relax into the ride. She was a sweet weight against his back. They traveled down empty streets, past buildings with gaping doorways and smashed windows. He circled around abandoned cars and bumped over rough ground.

"Squad Three, detour to the left," Indy said calmly.

Ash followed the order, but as they turned, he glanced to the right. Marin's sharp gasp sounded in his ear. In the distance, a lone canid stood in the middle of the street, its silhouette ominous and menacing. It was sniffing the ground, but a second later, it raised its huge head and looked in their direction. It had massive jaws, sharp teeth, and a row of wicked spikes along its back.

They turned down another street and lost view of it.

Ash's shoulders tightened, and he peered into every shadow, making sure there were no other hellish creatures around. It was only when they approached their destination that he relaxed just a fraction. They'd been lucky—not another creature, or a single raptor, the entire trip.

Ash hoped to hell their luck held the entire mission.

"Coming up on the tunnel entrance now," Indy murmured.

Ahead, the gaping mouth of the tunnel yawned open. It was larger than the entrance they'd used for the previous mission. Here, the roads leading in were a patchwork of cracks and potholes, but once, there would have been traffic pouring in and out of this tunnel. People heading into the heart of Sydney for business, shopping, and pleasure.

Some faded graffiti covered one wall. It consisted of stylized images of the raptors and their ships. Ash wondered if the artist had survived the invasion. He felt Marin's hands tighten on him.

Tane led them down to the tunnel's entrance, and they drove into the darkness.

Ash flicked on his night vision.

They moved slowly down the main tunnel. Overturned cars appeared out of the gloom, and Tane led them down a descending tunnel to the left.

"You need to keep tracking Marin's bot and follow its signal," Indy said.

"Acknowledged," Tane said.

Ahead, the eerie, red glow of raptor lighting filled the space. They moved deeper into the tunnel system.

"Squad Three...do you...signal breaking..." Indy's distorted voice came through the comm line.

Damn, they were losing her.

"On...your own...luck." Indy's voice cut off.

It was all up to them now. They slowly rode past a converging tunnel, and Ash heard the echo of guttural raptor speech. Marin shifted behind him, and he reached down and patted her gloved hand with his own.

"Raptor patrol ahead." Tane's near-soundless voice in the earpiece. "Stay quiet, and keep to the left."

The raptors appeared out of the gloom. They were standing around a drum that held a fire burning inside. They appeared at ease, although they all had their scaled weapons slung over their shoulders.

Ash's muscles tensed as they rolled past the aliens. One lifted his head, looking their way, like he sensed something. Ash watched the raptor as his bike rolled by, his breath tight in his chest. A moment later, one of the raptors said something, and the watcher turned to reply. Ash exhaled quietly.

Then the squad was past the raptors, and headed down another wide tunnel.

"This tunnel system is amazing," Marin said quietly. "A real engineering feat."

Ash knew it had been needed. After the United Coalition was formed, and Sydney declared the capital, the influx of business and people had exploded the population of the already overcrowded city.

Now, it was rotting, and home to an alien species intent on killing off humans once and for all. They'd already rounded up many of the survivors, and stuck them in alien labs—experimenting on them and turning humans into raptors.

No. They would never stop fighting back. And if Marin could hack the hub, it would give them another valuable weapon in their arsenal.

Besides, he thought, as he reached back and rested a hand on Marin's thigh, he sure as hell had something worth fighting for now. Marin was the bit of sweet he'd been missing all his life.

A loud, scraping noise caught his ear. The sound echoed through the tunnel and Ash frowned.

"What was that?" Marin whispered.

"Don't know."

The squad rounded another corner, and ahead, he saw a lone raptor standing in the middle of the tunnel. A big fucker, too. Close to seven feet tall.

It was just standing there.

"I don't like this." Hemi's near-silent murmur.

The raptor lifted something that it had been holding down beside its leg. Ash's gut cramped. It was a giant missile launcher.

And it was aimed straight at them.

"Fuck," Tane bit out. "They know we're here. Squad Three, evasive maneuvers."

Thump. Something shot out of the missile launcher. The projectile hit the ground only meters from the berserkers.

The missile exploded with a blinding flash. Flames roared up, filling the tunnel. Ash averted his gaze, and quickly flipped his night vision off to prevent blinding himself.

Shouts and guttural roars echoed off the walls.

"Ride! Get out of here," Tane shouted. "They know we're here but can't see us. They're firing blindly."

"Hold on," Ash yelled at Marin.

There was the sound of thunder made by boots on concrete, and in the next moment, an armed raptor patrol poured out of a side tunnel. Raptor poison splattered the walls, sizzling on contact.

Ash couldn't see his squad mates, but he heard them, and knew they were trying to ride out. Ash glanced over his shoulder, and saw more raptors jogging in from the way they'd come, canids loping at their feet.

"Keep moving forward!" Hemi's shout on the comm line.

Ash gunned his bike and shot forward. He dodged around a raptor and sped up.

He bit back a curse. The tunnel ahead was filled with raptors. Ash threw the bike left, then right, conscious of Marin tightly holding onto him. He weaved around raptors and other obstacles, feeling for a second like he was in a damn live-action version of Pre-Emptive Strike.

A stack of boxes appeared ahead, and with no time to swerve, he lifted the front wheels and he and Marin jumped them.

They landed with a bounce, following the rest of the berserkers deeper into the tunnel system. They raced through tunnels, heading down another ramp. If they were lucky, they could outrun these aliens, and still find a way to get Marin to the hub.

If they were unlucky, they'd die down here.

"What's that sound?" Levi asked.

Ash frowned and a second later, he heard it.

"It's flapping, like wings." Ash looked over his shoulder. There was something in the air, but he couldn't see anything.

"Fuck. What now?" Tane ground out.

"You see it?" Ash called out to Marin.

"No!"

Ahead, something came out of the darkness. There was a squeal of tires, and Ash knew someone had swerved to avoid the creature.

It was about the size of a dog, flying close to the top of the tunnel. It looked like a miniature version of the ships the raptors flew, that the humans had nicknamed pteros, after ancient pteranodons. But this one was more like a small, dinosaur-like bird, with leathery wings and a pointed beak. And it was carrying something in its claws.

As it passed over them, it made a loud squawk and released the red sphere it was carrying. The ball, covered in wicked spikes, hit the ground and rolled. *What the hell?*

Then Ash saw the ball start to glow red hot. "Bomb!"

He quickly jerked around the rolling object. It exploded behind them, and he heard Marin's muffled scream. Then the sound of gunfire echoed off the tunnel ahead. Some of his squad mates were firing.

That's when Ash saw more of the birds flying in their direction, each holding another bomb. A*ww, shit.*

He threw his bike to the right.

"Keep going," Tane yelled.

One of the balls hit the side wall of the tunnel and

exploded. Concrete and rock rained down. Ash accelerated. He had to get Marin out of there.

Another spiked ball dropped and bounced...right in front of them.

With a vicious curse, Ash yanked the bike to the left. Raptor fire opened up in the smoke billowing in the tunnel.

Then he heard Marin's scream—both in real life and through the comm line.

Her hands fell away from him and he felt her disappearing off the bike behind him. He tried to keep the bike steady with one hand, and reach back for her with the other.

He only felt empty air behind him.

"No!"

MARIN HIT the ground and all the air was knocked out of her.

She scrambled to her feet, chest heaving. She heard the alien poison that had hit her sizzling through her armor. *Dammit. Think, Marin.* She grabbed her water bottle off her belt, twisted the lid, and tipped water on the scorch mark over her ribs.

Instantly, the sizzling stopped. She breathed out in relief. It hadn't eaten all the way through the carbon fiber.

Then, she looked up and a rock of fear lodged in her belly. She was standing in the middle of smoke and flames in the center of the tunnel. Through the chaos, she saw the giant silhouettes of several raptors.

What she couldn't see were the berserkers.

Her breaths came in sharp pants. *Stay calm.* She pressed her hands together. No one could see her. She just needed to get out of the middle of the tunnel, and away from the raptors.

Then she saw her illusion flicker. *No. No!* She looked down and saw that the controls for the illusion had been hit by the poison.

The illusion flickered off.

The raptor closest to Marin spotted her. He lifted his gun and grunted. His demonic red eyes were on her as he aimed.

Terror flooded Marin. This was not Pre-Emptive Strike. There were no health packs if she went down. In real life, dead was dead.

Marin spun and ran. She charged through the smoke, trying to stay calm. In her head, she heard Ash's tense voice.

That's when she realized he was talking on the comm line.

"Marin! Where are you? Marin, answer me!"

A raptor appeared in front of her and Marin dived. She came up on her hands and knees, and scrambled forward.

"Use your thermo pistol, Marin. Then I can find you."

Thermo pistol. She pushed to her feet and pulled the weapon out of the holster with trembling hands. She spun and lifted it.

She fired off some wild shots. When she heard loud grunts, she turned and kept running. She rounded a sweeping corner in the tunnel. The thick smoke made her choke. God, how was she going to get out of here? How was she ever going to find the others?

"Marin!"

"Ash!"

"Where are you, Princess?"

Her throat was so tight. He was looking for her. "I don't know. All I see is smoke." She looked over her shoulder and gasped. Raptors were thundering toward her. "My God, more are coming. My illusion system failed."

"Run, Marin."

She did, leaping through the smoke. She needed a safe place to hide and she needed it now.

Then, out of the darkness, a huge shape reared up and let out a screech.

Marin froze in horror. It looked like a giant spider, the size of a small car, with two of its powerful legs waving madly in the air.

It was a creeper.

Marin tasted bile in her mouth, her gaze dropping to the creature's red, glowing belly. She knew that these beasts swallowed people whole and held them in their bellies, injecting them with Gizzida DNA and turning them into aliens.

Suddenly, a massive weight slammed into her back. She fell forward, crashing to the ground, her chin bumping the concrete. Pain exploded through her and she tasted blood in her mouth.

Raptor grunts sounded right above her. She looked up into the terrifying face of a raptor.

The massive alien stood. His chest was all gray scaly skin, and he wore metallic trousers and black boots. He reached down and grabbed her leg. Then he started dragging her down the tunnel.

A sob broke free of her chest. Oh, God, she was going to die.

She squeezed her eyes closed. She was never going to have the chance to be with Ash. To experience more mind-blowing sex, see him watching her with a sexy smile, to wake up beside him, to fall in love with him.

Her hands clenched, and she realized she was still holding her thermo pistol. Energized, she lifted it. Her arm was shaking badly, but she aimed in the general vicinity of the raptor. She pulled the trigger, thermo bullets firing in quick succession.

The raptor released her leg, and gore splattered her. The alien let out a deep, rasping scream, before dropping to the ground, claws tearing at his chest.

Marin froze, air heaving in and out of her lungs. She wanted to curl into a ball and hide, but that wasn't an option. She lifted her hand and swiped at the...she didn't want to think about what was coating her face and chest.

You can't hide, Marin. If you want to live, you have to find a way out.

She pushed to her knees. She was going to get out of here, dammit.

"Marin!"

She turned her head, and realized she'd heard his shout close by. She scrambled to her feet. "Ash, over here!"

She stumbled forward and saw a big, familiar shape coming through the smoke. *Thank God.*

"Thank fuck." Ash strode straight to her and scooped her off her feet. As he crushed her to his chest, she wrapped her arms around him and clung. Relief was a huge, shiny thing in her chest.

"God, Ash, I thought..."

"I've got you," he murmured.

"I was so afraid. I thought I was going to die."

"Found her." Levi appeared, clutching his carbine. "Fucking A. The others have cleared the area, but we won't have long before more raptors turn up." He looked over at the dead raptor on the ground and toed it with his boot. "You do that, Curls?"

She nodded.

Ash smiled. "Hell, Princess, you didn't need a rescue. You saved yourself."

She made a hiccuping sound. "Ash, I'm about two seconds away from a *major* meltdown."

He cupped her cheek, his finger brushing her skin. She realized he was rubbing away some gore.

"No, you're not," he said. "You're steady and smart and fierce."

Warmth rushed through her. She was starting to believe that he actually saw all of that in her.

Tane appeared, stomping up to them. "Connors, when I said don't rush off half-cocked, did you not hear me?"

"I couldn't leave her." Ash's arms tightened around her.

"We were coming back to get her," Tane said.

"Together. As a team. With a plan." Tane's dark gaze landed on Marin. "You okay, Marin?"

She managed a nod. "I am now."

"She sure is." Ash yanked her forward and slammed his mouth against hers.

Oh. Marin instantly forgot where they were and what had happened. She leaned in and kissed him back.

CHAPTER ELEVEN

He'd been so fucking afraid.

Ash opened his mouth, sliding his tongue against Marin's. She kissed him back eagerly, with no reservation. His. Alive. And in his arms. At the sound of a throat clearing, they broke apart.

Tane shook his head. "We have a mission. I need everyone back in the game. We need to get to that hub."

Ash nodded. The sooner they got the job done, the sooner he could get Marin out of this hellhole. He stroked a hand down her back. "Ready?"

He saw fear flash in her eyes, but then she set her shoulders back. "Ready."

Fucking fierce. He led her back down the tunnel with the others to where they'd stashed their bikes. He stepped inside the bike's illusion and helped her on behind him.

He pulled her arms snugly around him. "Hold on tighter this time."

She nodded against his back.

Once again, they were moving. This time, they traveled in single file, hugging one wall. In the distance, he could hear raptors. They knew his squad was in here, and they were searching for them.

A part of Ash wanted to turn his bike around and get Marin out. But she had a determined look on her face, and he knew her well enough to know that she was committed to seeing the mission through to the end.

Finally, Tane pulled them over. He was looking at the screen on his wrist. "We need to go through that doorway, and down some stairs." He pointed to a door set in the tunnel wall. "We'll pass through some maintenance corridors, and then we'll reach the spider bot's location."

And the hub.

They hid their bikes, leaving the illusion systems running. Then Hemi and Griff pried the door open. Soon, they were heading down a set of stairs. It was dark as hell, and Marin gripped his hand hard. But near the bottom, a dull, red glow filled the stairwell.

They stepped through a doorway and into a narrow corridor. Ash hissed out a breath.

More of those huge organic cables were running along the corridor. They were the same width as a man, pulsing, the red light in them glowing brighter with each pulse.

"Jesus," Marin breathed. Her expression was equal parts horror and curiosity.

"Come on." Tane stepped over a cable, and continued down the corridor.

Farther down the tunnel, Ash's boot stuck to the

floor. *What the—?* He lifted his boot, and eyed the ugly black crap on the cement.

"Sticky shit," Levi said, lifting his boot as well. "What the hell is this stuff?"

"Probably don't want to know," Dom drawled.

Tane clicked on a flashlight. All of them froze, and Marin gasped.

The floor, walls, and ceiling of the tunnel were covered in a sticky, web-like substance. Hemi reached up and touched it. It stuck to his glove like chewing gum.

"I don't like this," Hemi said.

Dom pointed. "Look."

Ash spotted the small, glowing, red pods dotted over the walls. They'd seen similar ones that were filled with animals, but these looked tiny in comparison.

Dom lifted his combat knife. He moved closer to the pod, leaning forward to study it.

Suddenly, the pod burst open and a black river of tiny insects poured out.

Except they weren't ordinary insects, they were alien insects.

More pods burst, and Ash shoved Marin behind him. A cloud of insects hit him in the chest and face, and he batted at them. He felt tiny stings as they nipped at his flesh. Around him, his squad mates were slapping at the bugs and swearing.

Ash swung his carbine around, and fired at the remaining pods on the wall. The rest of the squad started firing, too.

Levi let out a shout. Ash slapped more insects off his face, felt them trying to crawl into his nose and mouth.

Through the curtain of critters, he saw his friend had fallen. A giant swarm of the insects engulfed Levi. The man was thrashing around on the ground.

Hell, no. Ash stumbled over to his friend, and thrust a hand through the insects. They'd chewed through his glove, and he felt them nipping at his skin.

"Watch out," Marin yelled.

Ash saw a blinding blue light fill the tunnel. Marin was holding up her portable comp, and a bright blue light was coming from it.

The alien insects all swarmed for it. Ash's pulse raced. *Marin.*

She set her comp screen down and stepped back. The insects covered the light in a writhing mass. Marin calmly tossed a cedar oil grenade into the center of the tiny creatures.

Thwump. The grenade exploded, and the evergreen scent filled the air, along with a mist-like spray.

Some of the insects shriveled up and died, while the bulk of them scuttled away into the darkness.

Ash reached down for Levi. His friend grabbed his hand and Ash yanked him up. Levi uttered a stream of curses, spitting out insects. His cheeks were covered in blood.

"Good work, Marin." Ash grinned at her.

"How did you know it would work?" Tane asked, slapping at the last few insects on his armor. He was bleeding from above his left eye.

"I set my comp to emit a bright light, including some ultraviolet, which attracts insects. Like on a bug zapper." She scooped up her comp, checking it over. It was covered in a heavy-duty case and not damaged. "I made an educated guess about the cedar oil grenade. I've been reading some of Doc Emerson's notes on how she believes the cedar oil affects alien physiology—"

Ash yanked her into his arms and kissed her. "I love it when you talk geek."

She smiled, then she looked past him, her eyes widening. "Look."

She wriggled to get down and hurried past Ash. The cables traveling along the corridor turned downward, disappearing through the floor.

He moved up beside her and glanced down. It looked like some sort of access tunnel, which was clogged with the alien cables.

He studied the opening, and spotted a metal ladder attached to the side of the vertical tunnel.

Marin tucked her comp screen away and lifted her gaze to Ash's. "We need to go down there."

THE SQUAD'S boots echoed on the rungs of the ladder as they all descended into the darkness.

Marin was in the middle of the group. Tane had taken the lead, followed by Hemi, and then Ash. She was wedged between Ash and Levi. Griff and Dom were bringing up the rear.

The men were tense and quiet. It was so damn dark. She had the night vision lens over her left eye, but she wasn't used to looking at everything in shades of green. It was disorienting.

Then she heard Tane and Hemi talking in low-pitched tones. They'd reached the bottom.

A moment later, strong hands gripped her waist and pulled her off the ladder. Ash set her down, and she took a second to find her bearings. She looked around and realized that they were standing in a large underground room. There was a noticeable humming sound, and ahead lay a massive pile of cables. They were piled on top of each other and tangled. It almost looked like an ugly vine had grown out of control.

"Take a look around," Tane said. "But be careful."

Marin checked her comp screen. "The spider bot is in here somewhere." She stepped over some cables, staying close to Ash. "If you find anything that looks like a computer interface, he's likely to be there."

The men fanned out.

Marin stepped over another cable, searching the space. She spotted some old equipment, rusted and dented, but didn't see anything that looked like an alien interface. She poked around. "This looks like the controls for part of the ventilation system for the tunnels."

"Hey." Griff turned around, his face hardening. "Something touched my leg."

Everyone turned around, searching the green-tinted darkness. All Marin saw was the tangle of cables all over the floor. Then she caught movement out of the corner of her eye. She turned, peering into the shadows. *There.* Something was moving. She heard the sound of a body dragging over the ground.

"There's something moving over there in the darkness," she said.

The berserkers whipped their carbines up, moving forward. She felt the menace radiating off them.

Then she saw the movement again and her eyes widened. It wasn't *something*. It was the *cables*. "Watch out!"

One huge cable whipped up off the ground, like a giant snake. It waved around, just meters away. The squad shouted, and carbine fire sounded, lighting up the space. Marin squinted at the bright flashes of green light.

Suddenly, another slightly slimmer cable lifted up and wrapped around Marin like a rope.

What the hell? She struggled against the cable. She'd studied smaller versions in the lab, and knew they were blended with organic tech. But they merely carried power and information, they weren't alive.

Except somehow, these cables were sentient or programmed.

She would have found it fascinating, if the damn thing wasn't trying to squeeze her to death.

The cable moved again, and jerked her off her feet. A scream caught in her throat, and she found herself being waved around in the air.

"Marin!" Ash shouted.

There were more shouts and carbine fire. Suddenly, the cable tightened, starting to squeeze her in its grip. Pain grew in her chest. "Stop." The word came out as a whisper.

"It's crushing her." Ash's deep voice reverberated off the walls.

Tears welled in Marin's eyes. The pain was horrible. All she wanted was Ash. His arms around her, his big body against hers. She did not want to die when she'd only just found him.

Dammit, she wanted to live.

Marin struggled, fighting through the pain. The cable tightened more and her vision wavered.

Then the cable jerked. She opened her eyes, fighting to focus. She saw Ash leap up on the cable, climbing toward her. He was holding a huge combat knife.

He ran up the cable and when he reached her, he crouched down.

"You came for me," she said.

"I told you I was your own personal super soldier. Hold on, I'm getting you out of there." He lifted the knife and stabbed at the cable.

The cable started waving wildly through the air. Ash stabbed again, using the knife to hold onto the cable. Behind him, Marin saw more of the cables rising up and waving around. They were starting to look like the tentacles of some giant octopus.

The cables shifted, and beneath them, she glimpsed a jagged hole in the concrete floor, as though acid had eaten through it.

All of a sudden, the cable around her loosened and she felt herself falling. She heard Ash's curse and saw him falling with her.

They were plummeting toward the hole in the floor.

Marin screamed. As they shot downward, Ash's arms wrapped around her.

ASH CRASHED INTO A SPONGY CABLE, Marin landing on top of him. *Shit.*

He wrapped his body around Marin's, as they rolled and finally hit concrete. Ash shifted and sat up.

"Marin?"

"I'm okay." She sat up, looking a little dazed.

Ash touched her cheek, needing to feel her skin. "Anything hurting?" The damn alien cable had squeezed her hard. She could have broken bones or internal bleeding. He patted down her armor, checking for any cracks.

"Everything's hurting. But it isn't so bad now."

Her armor was intact, so it had protected her from the worst of it. He pulled out his flashlight, and clicked it on. He shone it around. There were cables everywhere—down the walls, across the floor. Thankfully, these fuckers weren't moving.

He aimed the light up, and his jaw tightened. The cables had moved again, and completely covered over the hole they'd fallen through. They were cut off from the others. He touched his ear. "Tane? You there?"

Nothing.

"Tane? Squad Three?" Ash shook his head. "Comms are cut off."

"Look at that." Marin scrambled up and moved across the space.

That's when Ash spied a glowing box. It was made of a tough, black substance, and covered with red lights.

"That what you've been looking for?"

She nodded. "It's an access point to the hub. And look. Hello, little guy."

Ash spotted the spider bot, its body pressed flat

against the base of the box. Marin pulled out her portable comp screen, and pressed something against the box.

Moving closer, Ash gripped his carbine—which he thankfully hadn't lost in the fall. He kept a close eye on the nearby cables. He wasn't taking any chances.

He watched Marin totally lose herself in her work. She tapped at the screen, the light illuminating her face. As she worked, her muscles relaxed. She was completely in the zone.

He loved watching her use that big brain of hers.

"If the aliens hadn't invaded, what would you be doing?" he asked.

She looked up. "I had my own startup company. We were making cutting-edge, experimental tech." A distant look crept into her eyes, a smile on her face. "It was a fun, creative place to work. I was set to be a millionaire."

He could see it. And it reminded him that she was way out of his league.

"But I don't dwell," she said. "Wherever we are, whatever we're doing, I know we have to find the good, enjoy it, protect it. We still have good here, right?"

He stared at her face. "Right."

"And you? What would you be doing?"

Ash shrugged. "I've no idea. I tried a lot of things, and most of them didn't work out, except for the Iron Kings." He thought of the brothers who hadn't made it. "I don't dwell, either."

"I know what you'd be doing." Marin paused her tapping. "You'd be riding a sexy motorcycle around, and be surrounded by gorgeous women."

Ash put a finger under her chin, tilting her head up to

meet his gaze. "There's only one gorgeous woman I'm interested in."

She stared at him for a second before she looked back down at her screen. "I might be starting to believe you."

She kept working, and Ash looked up, wondering what the hell his squad mates were doing. They had to be fighting to find a way in. Ash felt sweat beading on his face. In fact, the temperature had risen, and he felt a trickle of sweat slide down his back.

He looked back at Marin, and saw she was breathing heavily.

Shit. That was it. There was no air down here.

"I'm in!" Marin bounced on the balls of her feet like an excited kid. "All the way in. We can access the data, and have the spider bot relay it back to the Enclave. There are still a few hoops to jump through, but I've opened the door."

He smiled. "I appreciate the non-techspeak. Good work, Marin. I never doubted you."

Her gaze narrowed on his face. "What's wrong?"

So much for his poker face. "There's no air getting down here."

Her mouth dropped open. "No air?" Her chest heaved and she swiped a hand over her sweaty brow. "God. You mean we're going to suffocate?"

"MY SQUAD WILL FIND a way to get us out," Ash said.

Marin felt panic trickling into her veins. All the

elation at accessing the alien data hub evaporated. "I don't want to die."

He gripped her arms. "We are *not* going to die."

"I...I want to get this data. I want us to beat the aliens. I want..."

He stepped closer. "What do you want, Marin?"

If they were going to die, she may as well be truthful. "You." She swallowed. "I want you."

"Princess." His voice was a slow, sexy drawl.

"I like sex. I wasn't sure I was very good at it, but with you...it's *so* good."

"Marin—"

"But I don't just want you for hot sex. You're smart, and brave, and I just want you, Ash."

"Feeling's mutual, Princess. I want you naked in my bed. I want you begging for my cock. I want to sit beside you in the lab and watch you work."

She licked her lips and his gaze zeroed in on the movement. He groaned.

Her chest felt tight, and she had to fight to drag in a deep breath.

"Hey, relax." He wrapped an arm around her and pulled her down to sit on the floor. Then he looked at the cables. "I'll see if I can find a way out."

She watched him try to climb up higher, poking at the cables. None of them budged. Then he pulled out his carbine, aimed, and fired.

A cable shot out and slammed into Ash. It sent him flying.

"Ash!"

"I'm okay." He pushed to his feet. He lifted his weapon, and tried again.

Another cable whipped up and tried to wrap around him. Ash dodged and rolled. The cable settled back to the floor.

"They must be programmed to protect themselves," she said.

Ash muttered something under his breath, and headed back to her.

"What if we die here?" she said quietly.

"Not gonna happen," he growled. He tugged her onto his lap and kissed her.

Instantly, all the thoughts rushed out of her head. She pushed into him, kissing him back. Her hands crept up into his hair.

She was completely lost in the kiss. Lost in him.

"You'll just have to keep kissing me," she murmured against his lips. "To keep me calm."

He laughed. Such a good, sexy sound. "I could do that."

"And I'll try not to think about sitting among giant, killer alien cables and running out of air."

"Hey. Good thoughts, remember." He nipped her lips.

"Good thoughts. Right." She closed her eyes. "I'll think about sex, instead. With you."

He laughed again. "God, you're something, Marin."

The minutes ticked by, and soon she found herself blinking. She was so tired. She leaned into Ash, resting her head on his broad shoulder. "You're sure they'll come?"

He tugged her close. "Absolutely."

"I could fall in love with you," she said.

He jerked. "Princess—"

Her eyelids were too heavy to keep open. She probably shouldn't have made that confession to a bad-boy biker like Ash, but she was too tired to care. Besides, she was pretty sure she'd already started falling for him.

"No, Marin. Stay awake."

She mumbled something. Then, an annoying buzzing sound reached her ears. She had no idea what it was, but at this point, she was past caring.

The sound grew, and suddenly, something splattered down from above, hitting the floor nearby. Ash jumped to his feet, pulling her with him. Now she realized it was a sharp, buzzing sound.

As the cables shifted again, Ash dived on top of her, covering her with his body. They both looked upward.

Marin watched as a chainsaw cut through the cables above.

"Woo-hoo!" A wild shout. A hunk of cable fell down, flopping on the floor. Other cables pulled away, retreating.

Hemi's bearded face appeared in the gap above. "Anyone need a rescue?"

CHAPTER TWELVE

When the Hawk landed at the Enclave, Ash scooped Marin into his arms and carried her off the quadcopter.

"Taking her to the infirmary," he bit out.

Tane nodded. Ash didn't say anything, just dodged around Holmes, Noah, and Elle, and stalked out. He took the shortest route to the infirmary.

"Ash, I'm okay—"

He ignored her. "Getting you checked out. End of story."

"Bossy biker," she huffed.

"That's right."

He marched into the infirmary and saw Doc Emerson's head jerk up, her blonde hair swinging around her pretty face. She was standing near a row of bunks. One was occupied by an older woman with a bandage over her eye.

"Marin needs to be checked," he said. "She took a fall

off a bike, got squeezed by giant alien cables, and she was oxygen deprived for several minutes."

"Busy day." The doc's white lab coat flared out as she hurried over.

"I'm fine," Marin said again, sounding pissed. "And you fell too, and broke my fall, and had low oxygen, as well."

Doc Emerson looked from Marin to Ash and back again. She looked like she was fighting a smile. She nodded to one of the beds. "Set her down here."

Ash obeyed, ignoring Marin's glare. She subsided, and let the doc check her over. The doc's face turned focused and she waved a scanner over Marin.

Ash leaned against the wall. *Fuck.* When Marin had fallen off the bike, he'd never, ever felt the level of fear that had consumed him at that moment.

Then watching her being squeezed to death by the cables... He'd been frantic and helpless, and he hadn't liked it one fucking bit. He blew out a breath, and ran a hand through his hair. Caring for a woman was hell on a guy.

Emerson stepped back. "She's in perfect health."

Thank fuck.

"Told you," Marin said primly.

"A few bruises and scrapes," Emerson added. "But that's it." Then, the doc tried to run the scanner over Ash, without success.

He sidestepped and snatched Marin off the bed. "Thanks." He strode out.

"You're welcome," Emerson called out after them.

Levi was waiting in the hall. He'd stripped his upper

armor off and his T-shirt was lined with sweat. "Everyone okay?"

"I was okay before we went in there," Marin said. "But no one's listening to me."

"Glad you aren't hurt, Marin," Levi said. "You fucking held your own out there tonight."

Marin's cheeks pinkened. "Thanks."

Levi looked at Ash. "The general wants a debrief."

"Later," Ash said.

"He's a general, brother. He doesn't like to be kept waiting. Especially when the fate of the world is on the line."

"Marin got into the hub. She said the data will start to flow soon."

Marin nodded. "He's actually—"

Ash cut her off. "For now, she needs rest."

Levi grinned. "That what they're calling it these days?"

"Fuck you, King."

"No, thanks. You're not really my type."

"I can walk," Marin said with a sniff.

"No," Ash growled and stalked down the corridor.

Ash realized he was in full caveman mode, but he didn't care. Marin was *his*. He'd claimed her. He was going to make sure she was fed, watered, rested, and well fucked.

When he reached the door to her quarters, he waited while she unlocked it. He carried her inside, and set her on her feet.

"Comp, lights on," she said. "Low level."

Lights clicked on around the room. "Nice."

"I've added some tech I've been playing with."

"Go. Take a shower. I'm going to head to my room to shower, then get some food from the kitchen."

"Oh." Her face fell. "Right. Thanks for saving me—"

He gripped her chin. "You held up out there, Marin. You did your job, and you were fucking fierce."

She blushed prettily. "Thanks."

"Now, get your sexy butt in the shower. I'll be back in fifteen minutes."

She startled. "You will?"

He stepped closer until the toes of his boots bumped hers. "Yes, Marin. You're mine. Got it?"

"Got it," she whispered.

"Good." He stalked out of her room before he grabbed her, stripped her naked, and tossed her on the bed. Back at his place, he called the kitchen to order food, then started stripping off his armor. He took a quick shower, washing the stains of the mission away. He didn't want to go to Marin with any of it still on him.

But even after the shower, he felt edgy and energized. *Marin.* He needed Marin. He wanted to hear her sweet cries, feel her tight body clamp down on his cock, hear her heart beating under his ear.

He pulled on jeans and a well-worn Harley Davidson T-shirt he'd managed to save from before the invasion. After a quick trip to the kitchen to pick up a tray, he headed back to Marin's.

When he knocked on the door, she answered it, only wearing a towel. Her damp hair looked longer when wet, her curls tamed for the moment. She held the door open. "I didn't know what to wear. I—"

He slammed the door behind him and set the tray down. "You hungry?"

"Not really."

"Good." He spun, picked her up, and slammed his mouth down on hers.

She tasted so good. Fresh, clean, alive. She'd brushed her teeth, and she tasted like mint, and smelled like lemons. Sweet, sweet, Marin.

He angled his head, tongue sliding into her mouth. He knew he was edging on rough, but he couldn't make himself be gentle. Not this time.

He pushed her so she fell back on the bed, and then he stripped the towel off her. This time, she was watching him with a hungry gaze, and didn't try to cover herself.

Ash moved to sit near the head of the bed and tore his shirt over his head. He shoved a pillow behind his back and leaned against the headboard. Marin was watching him curiously.

"Touch yourself," he growled.

"What?"

"For weeks, I've sat in my room, knowing you were stroking yourself. Drove me out of my mind. I want to see it."

White teeth sank into her bottom lip, but she lifted a hand and slid it down her belly. Ash felt his muscles tense, and watched as her fingers brushed through the curls between her legs.

"Open your legs, Marin. I want to see it all."

She let them fall open, her mouth parting. Her fingers brushed through her folds. Her touch was tentative at first, but when she saw he was riveted, her desire amped up a notch and she lost her inhibitions. Her hips were shifting and he watched her fingers moving in circles over her clit.

Her moan echoed around them and then she slid a finger inside herself.

Fuck. Ash's cock was rock-hard, pulsing in his jeans. "You are so fucking gorgeous."

Her skin was flushed and her fingers went back to rubbing her clit.

"Good girl. Now I want you to come and say my name when you do."

MARIN HAD NEVER FELT SO sexy or so alive.

Sensations were burning through her, and with every stroke, she felt her orgasm looming. Ash's gaze was on her, hot and burning.

This outrageously sexy man had protected her, saved her, helped her do her job, and now was looking at her like she was the sexiest thing he'd ever seen.

Her release hit her and she cried out Ash's name. She felt her legs shake and her back arched. She rode through the wave of pleasure.

When she could finally see again, she turned on her side and her belly clenched.

Ash had opened his jeans and shoved them down. His beautiful cock was free and he was stroking himself. When he looked up, his face was set in hard lines.

"You want this, Princess?" He stroked his cock again. She nodded.

"Climb aboard."

Heat rushed into her cheeks but she crawled up the bed toward him. He pulled her into his lap, clamping his hands on her hips. Then he helped lower her down on his cock.

"Holy fuck," he bit out.

"Oh," she breathed. "You feel so big this way." She pressed her hands to his shoulders for leverage.

"Keep going, Princess. You can take me." He said the words through gritted teeth.

She moaned, her body sliding down around his cock. The stretch was the perfect balance between pleasure and pain. Her breasts bobbed in front of his face, and he leaned forward and sucked one nipple into his mouth.

Her hands flexed on his shoulders, and she sank down another inch. Then another. His hands dug into her hips.

"I'm so full," she moaned.

"Ride me, Marin." He moved her hips.

She took over, rocking on his cock and finding her rhythm. Soon, she was slamming down on him hard. So. Good. "I like this. Oh, God."

He slid his hands around to clench her ass, driving her on. "Any time I'm inside you, I like it. Hell, even when I'm not inside you, I like it, too."

She kept moving up and down, whimpering with pleasure.

His gaze dropped. "I love watching you take my cock." He slid a hand between her legs, and rubbed a knuckle over her clit.

She gasped. "Oh, I'm going to come again."

"So come, Princess."

The pleasure built, and then cascaded over her in a rush. Her nails bit into his skin and she cried out his name.

Ash sank a hand into her hair, pulling her head back. "I want a clear view of your face, Marin. Give it all to me."

Suddenly, he pulled her off him. As his cock slid out of her, she cried out. "No."

He spun her around on her hands and knees. When his hands cupped her ass, she went still. Then she felt the fat head of his cock notch between her folds. Before she could prepare, he slammed inside her.

"Oh!" Marin dropped her head down to the covers. He was rough and she liked it.

"Need to fuck you. Mark you." His skin slapped against hers. "Look at that pretty back and upturned ass. All mine."

The next orgasm came out of nowhere. Marin gave a shocked, choked cry.

Ash's thrusts got harder, jerkier. "I'm gonna come, Princess." He lodged himself inside her and groaned. "Fuck. Gonna pour everything I've got into your hot, little body."

Marin was wrecked. She had her cheek to the covers, her ass still in the air and Ash was still inside her. She could hear the air sawing in and out of him. Felt the perspiration sticking them together.

Then he pulled out, and she moaned. She felt one strong hand on her thigh and looked back. God, he was looking at her. She should be embarrassed, but she felt too good to care.

"Watching my come slide down your thighs." He smiled. "Marked. Mine."

Marin quivered. This harder, rougher, rawer Ash was new. And sexy as hell.

He climbed off the bed and went into the bathroom. When he came back, she hadn't moved far, just dropped down into a sprawl. He leaned over her and she felt a warm, wet washcloth stroke between her legs. She made a small sound, but didn't move.

"I'm wrecked," she murmured. "Think I'll sleep for a week."

He chuckled and went to discard the cloth. He'd just sat on the edge of the bed, and Marin was fighting off taking a nap, when a loud *ding* came from a tablet resting on the bedside table. Marin scrambled up like she'd been hit with a shockround.

"Apparently, you aren't quite as wrecked as you thought," Ash said dryly.

She snatched up the tablet, the light illuminating her face. She scanned the data.

"I probably shouldn't mention the sexy picture you make, naked in the center of the bed, hunched over your comp screen."

"Ash!" Then she grinned. "We got through! We're getting alien data." Her gaze flicked up and met his. "I need to get to the lab."

Ash nodded. "Let's go." He grabbed his jeans off the floor.

She threw her legs over the edge of the bed and

paused. Her gaze was running over his body. "Um, sorry."

He paused. "For what?"

"Well, we were, um—"

"Fucking each other's brains out?"

"Right. And now I want to rush off to work."

He cupped her cheeks. "Marin, your work is important, and you're good at it."

Her insides softened. "I keep thinking you're too good to be true."

He released her to pull his T-shirt over his head. "Nah. I'm going to have you make it up to me later by sucking my cock."

Her mouth opened, her gaze dropped to his fly, and desire flickered in her belly.

Ash looked like he was fighting back a smile. "Alien data. Lab."

"Work. Right." She pushed off the bed with a wide smile.

CHAPTER THIRTEEN

In the lab, Marin leaned forward over her computer, tapping as fast as she could. There was *so* much data here and more was pouring onto the screen every second.

Elation flooded her. There was a lot of stuff that needed translating and that would take time, but it was very possible that this could help them beat the Gizzida, once and for all.

She shifted on her chair, and felt an ache between her thighs. It was a reminder that the reason for that was sitting right beside her, his big body sprawled in the chair, watching her. Damn, he looked so good. She shivered.

He leaned over, pushing her curls to the side, and pressed a kiss to the back of her neck. "How's it going?"

Desire swirled through her. "Great. Awesome."

"I love watching you work. It makes me hard."

Her gaze dropped to his lap, and sure enough, she saw the bulge straining against his zipper. "Is it like this all the time?"

"Don't know. Never had it happen like this before."

A quiver went through her. "For me, too."

He grinned at her. "How's it going with the data?"

Data? Marin shook her head. "Data, right." She looked at the raptor language filling the screen. "There's a lot of stuff here. I can't read it all, so I'll have to let the translation program and Elle Steele help." Something caught Marin's eye. "Oh, my God." She moved her head from side to side as she scanned the information.

Ash straightened. "What is it?"

"If I'm reading this correctly, we were right about the Gizzida having a single leader." She looked up at him. "And she's *here*."

"Shit. Really?"

Marin nodded. "I mean, on Earth. Well, okay, not *on Earth*, but on a ship that's in orbit."

Ash's face hardened. "So she's in charge of the invasion."

Marin stood, pulling a hard drive over. "I've got to get a copy of this, and get it all backed up."

The screen flickered and went blank, before coming back to life.

"What was that?" Ash asked.

She frowned. "I'm not sure. Maybe a power surge? I've never had an issue with my comp, and Noah's done all kinds of mods to keep the system stable." She tapped the keyboard, checking the system. "It seems fine now. I need to get the full translation program running, and then I'll run a diagnostic—"

A window popped up, and Marin scanned. Every muscle in her body tensed, horror seeping into her veins.

"Marin?"

"No, no, no." Her fingers flew across the keyboard. She reached up and swiped at the screen.

Ash stood, frowning. "Marin, what is it?"

She could barely hear him over the hard thump of her heart. This *couldn't* be right. "It looks like...I can't believe this." She shook her head. "This is all my fault."

He gripped the nape of her neck. "What?"

"The Gizzida are using my link to hack *our* system." *Oh, God.* "I have to shut it down."

"Do it."

She kept tapping. "I should have thought about this." Her fault. "I used some of their tech, and it must have given them a way in. I...can't shut it down. Come on!"

Suddenly, the lights and screens clicked off, plunging them into darkness. Marin stared into the thick, impenetrable black, her throat clogging with fear.

"Ash."

His big hand grabbed hers. "I'm here. The backup power will come on in a minute."

Sure enough, a few seconds later, red lights clicked along the walls. They cast a gloomy glow across the lab. She saw the comp screen flicker back to life.

That's when she heard the distant echo of screams from outside.

Ash shoved a chair back, staring at the door.

Marin rose, her stomach tying up in knots. "Oh, God, what's going on?"

They hurried to the door. Ash flung it open, and they stared at the waves of people running past. The screams were getting louder.

A muscled man charged down the corridor carrying a carbine. "Everyone get back in your rooms!" His gravelly voice reverberated off the walls. Marcus.

"Marcus, what's going on?" Ash asked.

"Connors, grab a carbine. All the squads are needed. The raptors have breached the northern end of the Enclave."

Shock rocketed through Marin. No.

Ash cursed. "Northern end is the storage and the new quarters that are currently being built."

Marcus nodded. "No one living there. Anyone in the area has been evacuated, but people in the main part of the base are panicking."

"This is my fault." Marin wrapped her arms around her middle. "They piggybacked in on my hack, and that must have been how they found the door and got inside."

"We had no warning." Marcus' scarred face looked savage. "The drones didn't pick them up, or the cameras. They dodged our patrols."

All her fault. Bile filled her throat. "They got into the system and manipulated our security."

"And they did a dry fucking run the other day," Ash bit out. "When they attacked Eric and Marin."

"From what we can tell, it's a small team," Marcus said. "They haven't made it into the main part of the Enclave, and security has initiated a partial lockdown. The squads are going in to take these bastards down."

Ash nodded. "I'll get my weapon."

"We're going in blind," Marcus said grimly. "Raptors have locked us out of the system in that area. The team in the Command Center are managing to keep them out of the rest of the Enclave system."

Marin spun and raced over to her desk. She snatched up her tablet. She quickly linked up and came up against the alien firewall. *Oh, no you don't.*

She tapped, typing in commands, and when she hit another wall, she decided that instead of going around it, she'd go under it.

Bingo. "I can access cameras in the northern area." Images filled the screen, and instantly, she saw a group of raptors marching through an empty Enclave corridor. "Look." She tilted the screen.

"Brilliant," Ash said.

Marcus nodded. "Good work. Can you patch it through to the Command Center?"

She nodded.

"What's that raptor doing?" Ash asked.

Marin looked at the screen. She saw a raptor plugging something into a control panel on the wall. "Oh, no."

"What?" Marcus demanded.

"He's trying to break through to the rest of the Enclave system." She tapped the screen, zooming in. "If he gets in, he'd have full control of the Enclave."

"Can you block him?" Ash asked.

She nodded. "I can try." She started tapping furiously.

The sound of running footsteps reached them. Noah appeared, his dark hair pulled back and tied at the back of his neck. His shirt only had two buttons done up. "What the hell is going on?"

"The Gizzida piggybacked my link," Marin said. "They hacked *us*."

"Fuck." Noah pressed a hand to the back of his neck.

She knew he understood the full implications.

"A team of raptors are in the northern end of the Enclave," Marcus said. "We've blocked them in, but Marin says there is one trying to break through the system."

Noah shouldered his way past, and dropped down behind his computer. "Let me see if I can stop the asshole."

Marin watched him get to work. Noah was a genius, and his face turned hard and focused as he worked.

Noah cursed. "This bastard is good."

Marin leaned over his shoulder. "The only way to keep him out and cut their connection to our system is to shut down the system in the northern end of the Enclave."

"We can't do that from here," Noah said.

She nodded. "I need to go in and do it. This is my fault, and I want to fix it."

"No," Ash said.

"You couldn't have predicted this, Marin," Noah said angrily.

"Maybe not," she said. "But I sure as hell can fix it."

"No, you're not going in there," Ash ground out. "You'll stay here. Safe."

She lifted her chin. "Ash, I have to do this."

"I already fucking took you into raptor territory, and you nearly died!"

"I came back with a few bruises."

"I'll go," Noah said.

Marin shook her head. "I forged the link, and we both know I'm better at this kind of work." She looked back at Ash. "Are you going to lock me up? Take away my choices? Make me feel like I can't do my job? Should I not be me and just sit around wringing my hands?"

"Fuck." Ash kicked a chair and sent it spinning across the lab.

"Ash," Marcus said. "I know it sucks, but we need her. You protect her. You keep her safe, and let her do what she needs to do."

Ash looked at Marin, his jaw tight. "You stay beside me every second of the mission. You do exactly what I say."

Marin nodded.

Ash muttered one more curse before he grabbed her hand. "Come on. Let's do this."

ASH MOVED with his squad down the empty corridor, the red emergency lights giving the place a creepy glow. There hadn't been time for full armor, so he only wore his chest plate. He held his carbine, had a pistol on his side and his gladius combat knife strapped to his thigh.

Marin was in the center of them, her face set. She carried her portable comp clutched to her chest. He wished he could have decked her out in full armor, but he'd only had time to shove a thermo pistol at her so she was at least armed.

"Wait for me," came a deep voice from behind them.

As one, they spun, and saw a large silhouette appear out of the darkness. He was holding a big, heavy assault carbine, which was twice the size and weight of a regular carbine, and packed three times the punch. Ash saw the butts of two more rifles protruding over his broad shoulders, strapped to his back.

"Manu, you aren't cleared for missions," Tane said.

"I'm not cleared to go in the field because of this hunk of metal." Manu tapped his leg, and they all heard the dull *thunk* of his prosthetic. "But I'm not an invalid. I fucking taught you to shoot, and I'm going to protect our home."

Ash knew Manu was a hell of a soldier. If he hadn't have lost his leg on a mission last year, he'd still be a berserker. Hell, he *was* still a berserker.

Finally, Tane nodded. "Let's go. More raptors have followed the initial team in. Squad Nine and Hell Squad have engaged. The bastards are tearing through the storage areas, and setting the place alight."

"God," Marin murmured, her chin dropping to her chest.

Ash touched her arm. "Fire can't get through the lockdown to the rest of the Enclave." But he was aware if they lost all of their supplies—food, medicine, clothing, artwork—that it would hurt.

He saw that Marin was blaming herself for this. It was stamped all over her face.

They reached the lockdown gate. A giant steel door had slammed down, closing off the corridor. A small door set in the center of the metal was closed and guarded by Captain Kate Scott, and a team of her security guards.

The captain nodded at them. She didn't look like she'd been dragged from her bed for an emergency. Her dark hair was pulled back and her fatigues neatly pressed. "We'll let you through and then shut the gate behind you. You know that if you come back to the gate with even just one raptor behind you, I can't open it."

Tane nodded. "We know the drill."

Her gaze landed on Manu. "I don't believe you're authorized for this mission."

Manu lifted his assault carbine. "This is my authorization."

She stared at him for a moment, before she gave a small nod. She looked at one of her guards, and the woman pulled the heavy, reinforced-steel door open.

"Good luck," Kate said.

Ash helped Marin through the door. Once they were all on the other side, the door swung closed with an ominous *clang*. The berserkers started forward, carbines up.

They moved swiftly and quietly. The sounds of fierce fighting from up ahead reached them. Beside Ash, Marin stiffened.

"Remember, you stay back," he said.

She nodded, tugging at her shirt. Again, he wished he'd had time to get armor on her. But it didn't matter because he wasn't planning to let any raptors near her.

"Anything goes wrong, you head back to the gate."

"I will, Ash. And you stay safe, SuperSoldier."

He paused long enough to press a quick kiss to her lips. Then, they rounded a corner to find Hell Squad fighting a group of raptors.

"Stay back." Ash raced forward with his squad mates, and started firing.

He was angry. Angry that again, he had to risk Marin and put her in the line of fire of the Gizzida. Angry that the power-hungry bastards were relentlessly trying to kill innocent human survivors.

These damn aliens were like a horde of insects. They just kept coming and coming, to pick over every last bone.

He sighted the closest raptor and fired. He had a fair bit of anger to work off. He took down another raptor, and swung to face the next.

He watched Claudia come into view, firing her carbine. Beside her, huge Gabe was wrestling with another raptor. They swung around and Gabe, face emotionless, rammed the alien into the side of the corridor.

Ash fell into the familiar groove of fighting. He fired and kicked, taking down each giant alien that came up against him. But for the first time, he felt the warmth in his chest. He wasn't just fighting because he was a good killer. He wasn't fighting because this was all he had, all he knew. Now, he was fighting for his woman. For the bright, fresh woman who made it all worthwhile.

He swung around, firing at more incoming aliens. He gave a roar.

Beside him, Levi tossed a grenade. Ash watched it bounce into the center of the raptors.

"Fire in the fucking hole!" Levi shouted.

Boom. The contained explosion lit up the tunnel for a second, the ground shaking.

Then Manu stepped forward and dropped to one

knee. He lifted the heavy assault carbine and fired. Green laser poured out in a deadly rush.

"Ash!"

He spun to look back at Marin. She was pointing across the corridor. He glanced over and spotted the tech raptor—who was slimmer than the others and clutching the raptor version of a tablet—sneaking down a side corridor.

As Ash watched, Marin shimmied down along the corridor wall, then turned the corner, following the alien.

Fuck. Ash fired at the raptor right in front of him, then leaped over the downed body. He charged through the fight and raced after Marin.

Ahead, smoke billowed from the burning side rooms. He saw her slim form disappear, and then she was lost in the smoke.

Double fuck. He charged in after her.

CHAPTER FOURTEEN

She was going to stop this.

Marin hurried through the smoke, staying close to the wall. She'd let this happen, and she was going to stop it. This was their home, their sanctuary, and they weren't going to lose it.

Marin had just found something special, someone special, someone who liked her just the way she was. She was falling in love with Ash Connors and she wanted a chance to take that all the way.

She paused, listening for any sign of the raptor she'd seen sneak this way. Heavy footsteps. She peered through the smoke.

There. She saw the alien turn down another corridor.

She glanced back through the billowing smoke. Where was Ash? She'd let him know she was following the raptor, but she guessed he'd gotten caught up fighting off the raptor soldiers.

It didn't matter. She had to push forward. She

couldn't afford to let this raptor do any more damage than he already had.

Pulling out her thermo pistol, she crept down the corridor. Ahead, she heard a grunt. Through the smoke, she saw the shadow of the raptor as he held up a black tablet with jagged edges. He was standing beside an open Enclave control panel on the wall. As she watched, thin, worm-like wires snaked out of the tablet and stabbed into the control panel.

No, you don't. Steeling herself, Marin lifted the thermo pistol and strode forward. She pulled the trigger. Bullets slammed into the wall and the raptor ducked out of the way.

Up close, he towered over her, but Marin reminded herself that he wasn't a fighter. He was a geek, just like her. But she had a lot more to lose than he did.

She strode forward again, aiming at his chest.

Before she could pull the trigger, she heard a low, inhuman growl. The hairs on the back of her neck rose, and her heart knocked hard in her chest. Some part of her brain screamed at her to run.

A canid leaped out of the smoke, sailed over the crouched raptor, and jumped straight at Marin.

Shit. She stumbled backward and landed on her butt. The thermo pistol flew out of her hand and clattered on the ground nearby.

The canid skulked closer, making low growling sounds in its throat.

Marin scuttled backward, fear closing her throat. She reached out a hand, trying to find her pistol.

The alien dog's muscles bunched and it sprang forward.

She screamed, throwing her hands up to hold it off. The canid slammed into her, knocking her flat on her back. It pinned her to the floor, its claws clicking on the concrete floor on either side of her.

Marin's hands were pressed against tough scales. The beast opened its mouth, and the stench of rotting meat hit her, making her stomach heave. She choked back a sob, seeing the huge fangs just inches from her face.

Marin dropped a hand down by her side. She fumbled around and found the cedar oil grenade she had stuffed in her pocket.

The canid growled, the sound vibrating through Marin. She ripped the grenade from her pocket, just as the animal reared back, ready to clamp its huge jaws around her head. She thumbed the activation switch and thrust her entire arm into the creature's mouth, feeling the sting of razor sharp teeth tearing into her arm. She bit down on her lip and yanked her hand out. *Come on.*

The grenade exploded.

Cedar oil sprayed everywhere and the creature's body jerked. The oil filled the canid's mouth and covered Marin's face.

The dog leaped off her with a wild screech. As it danced in circles, shaking its head, Marin collapsed on the ground, sucking in air. She was drenched in cedar oil, which, she decided, was infinitely better than being chewed on by a canid.

Then a huge figure appeared above her.

The raptor.

Oh, no. She watched the alien lift a giant clawed hand up above his head, ready to slam it down on her. Her muscles bunched, and she desperately groped around on the floor. Where the hell was the pistol?

The raptor swung. Marin rolled to the side and the raptor's fist hit the ground. She saw the thermo pistol right in front of her face. She grabbed it, rolled, and fired.

Her aim was way off, but the bullet lodged in the raptor's shoulder. He let out a horrible, guttural roar.

"There's more where that came from, asshole," she yelled.

All of a sudden, carbine fire echoed off the walls, and green laser fire lit up the smoke-filled tunnel. The raptor's body jerked, laser fire tearing into him. He fell backward, and landed in a sprawl on the floor.

Marin scrambled into a crouch and recognized Ash striding toward her. Sweet relief flooded her whole body. She leaped to her feet and ran at him. She launched herself into the air and he caught her with one arm, yanking her close.

Their kiss was fast and desperate.

"Did you see?" she said, adrenaline making her talk too fast. "I was badass."

"I saw, but no more missions," Ash ground out. "Ever. I'm keeping you naked in my bed."

She laughed, squeezing him tight. Then she pulled back. "I've got to see what he was doing."

Ash nodded and set her on her feet. She raced over to the raptor tablet, trying to make sense of the raptor characters. Several at the bottom of the screen were changing.

Like a countdown.

Her belly cramped. "I think he's uploading a virus to our system." She frowned. "It's still uploading."

"Can you stop it?"

"I don't know." Panic was like acid in her veins. She gripped the two black cables attaching the tablet to the wall. She tugged and tugged, but they wouldn't budge.

Ash grabbed them, and yanked. Nothing. "Fuck. Can we cut it?"

"It's too strong." Marin heard noises behind them. Tane and the rest of the berserkers appeared in the tunnel.

"We have another group of raptors incoming." Tane's face was set like stone. "We need to drop back and find some cover."

"I've got to stop this virus uploading." Marin tapped on the screen. "I think I can shut down the program, but I need more time."

Ash lifted his carbine. "We'll give it to you. You do your thing."

She drew in a shuddering breath. "Right."

He leaned down and pressed a hard kiss to her lips. "You can do this, Princess. I know you can."

Determination filled her. Ash Connors looked at her like she could do anything, and this was what Marin was best at.

She might not be PrincessBadass with a carbine, but she sure as hell was PrincessBadass with a comp. She nodded and bent over the tablet.

Time to show the raptors how it was done.

ASH STARED down the smoke-filled tunnel, waiting. Around him, his squad did the same thing, weapons up and gazes unwavering.

The raptors were close. Ash could sense them.

He glanced back at Marin. She was absorbed in her work, and had her own tablet joined up to the raptor one. The dead raptor lay nearby, and a flash of pride filled him. His fierce PrincessBadass.

"Another berserker takes the fall," Levi said. "Ash Connors in love. I always knew you'd score a gorgeous babe, just never guessed it would be a geek hottie."

Ash grinned. "It's fucking awesome, man."

"Hell, yeah," Hemi said. "I get to have the sexiest woman in the world in my bed every night. And wake up with her lips wrapped around my—"

"We get it," Ash said. "And if Cam hears you talking like that, you might wake up on the couch."

Hemi's grin widened. "But it's more than just the hot sex. It's the whole package. Hell, Cam's smile makes everything worth it."

Yeah, Ash knew exactly what Hemi was talking about. *Shit*. Ash controlled a jolt. He was in love with sweet, smart Marin Mitchell.

Levi slapped Ash's back. "I know you reached for more once, and life kicked you in the teeth. I'm glad you weren't afraid to reach again. If I find a woman who looks at me like Marin looks at you..."

Suddenly, the lights came back on.

"Woo-hoo," Hemi called out. "Nice job, Curls."

Marin looked up, smiling. "You're welcome. And I've got the virus contained! I can't shut it down, but I've got it quarantined. With Noah's help, we might be able to study it."

Ash grinned at her. "Brilliant."

She took a little bow.

There was a hint of movement in the smoke right behind Marin. Ash frowned.

"What the fuck is that?" Tane called out.

Ash swiveled to look in the opposite direction.

A group of raptors was moving down the tunnel. They were huddled together, all holding metallic shields up and interlocked. They looked like a giant, armored animal moving down the corridor.

"Marin!" Ash swung back to her. "Get over here."

But as he yelled, his squad opened fire, and she didn't hear him. She was pulling her tablet toward her, disconnecting from the raptor tech.

Again, he saw something move behind Marin.

"Marin!" Ash charged toward her, whipping his carbine up. Levi turned to look at him.

Marin lifted her head, staring straight at Ash. A giant raptor charged out of the smoke behind her.

Fuck. Ash didn't have a shot. "Marin, get down!"

The raptor moved and a huge black blade punched out through Marin's chest, just below her breasts. Her eyes went wide, and her comp dropped to the floor and shattered.

Not computing what he was seeing, Ash stared at the jagged black edge of the sword protruding through her.

The raptor had stabbed her with a sword.

"No!" Ash let out a roar, a red haze covering his vision. He rushed forward.

The raptor pulled the blade back, and with it gone, Marin slumped to the ground.

Ash opened fire. He held the trigger down, watching the laser tear into the raptor. The alien collapsed, but Ash kept firing, fueled by the hot, molten rage inside him.

Two more raptors materialized. Ash didn't care. He'd mow through every raptor on the planet if he had to. Anything to save Marin.

Suddenly, Dom stepped up beside him, wielding a shotgun. He held it up and it boomed as he fired.

One raptor stumbled back. On the other side of Ash, Levi appeared, his carbine roaring as he took down the other raptor.

Trusting his squad mates to take care of them, Ash dropped down beside Marin. He turned her over, cradling her in his arms. Blood soaked her clothes, her chest dominated by the terrible wound.

All around them, he heard shouting and weapons fire. Then he heard a gravelly voice.

"Hell Squad, ready to go to hell?"

"Hell yeah," a chorus of voices shouted. "The devil needs an ass-kicking!"

Hell Squad had arrived. But too late to help Marin.

Ash fought the horrible tearing inside him. "Marin." Her name was a broken plea.

AT FIRST, Marin felt a tearing, burning pain in her chest, but it had faded now. Now, she felt like she was floating.

Strong arms held her close and she looked up into Ash's face. Her pulse jumped. It was a terrible, pained mask.

"I'm here, Marin." His voice was ragged. He laid her down flat, his hands tearing at her shirt.

She watched as he pressed wadded fabric against her chest, and checked her pulse.

She liked seeing him use those medical skills he'd never had the chance to hone. She felt him pressing down hard on her chest, and she whimpered. That hurt. She decided to focus on his handsome face, instead. He would have made a hell of a doctor. A badass, tattooed doctor, who would have driven the nurses wild.

She smiled. And he'd wanted her. Who would have thought?

Then she saw tears in his eyes.

"Don't be sad." She wanted to touch his stubbled cheek, but her arm wouldn't move.

"Hold still," he said. "Tane, we need Doc Emerson."

"She's on her way," came Tane's deep voice. "Indy called her already."

A dull, heavy lethargy was creeping over Marin. It was strange, her eyelids were so heavy. She blinked slowly.

"You stay with me, Marin." One of Ash's hands touched her curls, then brushed down her cheek.

"No one has ever looked at me the way you do," she whispered.

A spasm crossed his face. "I'm going to look at you like that every day. Every damn day for the rest of our lives. You're mine, Marin."

Sweet pain burned through her. It was everything she'd ever wanted. "I never thought I'd have a sexy biker bad boy in my bed." She let her eyes close.

"No. Hold the fuck on, Marin." There was a hard edge to his voice, and so much pain. "I need my fierce fighter right now. Where's my badass princess?"

She managed to open her eyes, but it was a battle. "I love you, SuperSoldier." God, was that raspy whisper hers?

Ash's hand gripped hers, bringing it to his chest. "No, Marin. No."

But she couldn't keep her eyes open anymore. Darkness overtook her, and the last thing she heard was a horrible, anguished cry.

CHAPTER FIFTEEN

Ash stared at the blood on his hands. Marin's blood. He could still feel it pumping out of her as he'd put pressure on her wound. He could still feel it sliding down his arms as he'd tried to stem the flow.

He'd kept the pressure on until Doc Emerson and her team had arrived. They'd whisked Marin away on a floating iono-stretcher.

Jesus H. Christ. Ash pressed his hands against the wall outside of the infirmary. Every second, the image of that blade slicing through Marin replayed in his head.

He sensed a presence beside him, and a hand landed on his arm. He knew it was Levi.

"She's small, but she's way tougher than she looks," his friend said.

His squad stood around him, still covered in the sweat and grime of the fight. The raptors had been killed or contained, and the breach of the Enclave had been shored up.

Noah had sent a team to the tech lab to monitor the virus that Marin had contained. He was standing just down the hall, his face set in worried lines, with his woman, Laura, by his side. Several tech team members had come and gone, all of them were waiting for news on Marin.

"She is tough." His fierce princess. Ash's fingers curled. She'd be all right. She had to be.

"She must be brave to take you on," Hemi said.

Ash tried to smile, but couldn't quite do it. What if Marin didn't make it? *God. Fuck.*

It had been too long. Ash knew that if the doc had pumped Marin full of nanomeds, then the tiny medical machines would have finished healing her by now. Something was terribly wrong.

His head snapped up, and he stared at the closed door of the infirmary. It had been hours. He couldn't handle waiting any longer. He charged up to the door and banged it open. He dodged Levi, as his friend tried to grab him.

The infirmary was a hive of activity. Several people, including some squad members, had been injured in the attack.

Ash strode toward the surgery bays.

A short, round nurse with dark skin stepped in front of him and held up her hands. "Hold it right there, soldier."

"Move. I need to see her."

"She's still in surgery."

Still? His gut was as hard as stone. "How is she? What's her prognosis?"

A sympathetic look flickered over Norah's face. Ash knew what that meant, and it cut into him.

"No." He shook his head, refusing to believe it.

One of the surgical bay doors opened, and a weary-looking Emerson stepped out. Her scrubs were covered in blood. Marin's blood.

She looked at him and arched a brow. "Do I barge in when you're on a mission?" She walked over to a set of long sinks and started rinsing off her gloved hands.

There was so much blood. Ash felt a wave of dizziness hit him.

"Hey, easy there, big guy." Norah grabbed one of his arms and firm hands gripped the other. Ash looked into Levi's unsmiling face. They helped him into a chair.

Doc Emerson stepped in front of him and he stared her straight in the eye. "Is she dead?" His voice cracked.

Emerson sighed and sat down beside him. "No. I've done what I can. I gave her a large dose of nanomeds."

Hope flared inside him. She was alive and he knew that nanomeds could perform miracles.

"But they aren't working, Ash," the doc said gently. "There's too much damage."

His chest caved in, and he dropped his head into his hands. He was going to lose her. He sensed Levi staying close and noticed Tane right behind him. Ash knew they were there to lock him down if he started to lose his shit.

"The nanomeds are keeping her alive for the moment, but...I'm so sorry." Emerson pressed a hand to Ash's leg. "I wish there was more I could do."

Ash stared at the floor, images of Marin running

through his head. Her laughing, her concentrating, her crying his name in pleasure. Once again, life had given him a taste of sweet and good, and now it was going to tear it away from him. In the most bloody and painful way possible.

He lifted his head, and saw the rest of his squad standing nearby as silent support.

"Can I see her?" he asked Emerson.

The doctor nodded.

When Ash stepped inside the surgical room, Tane and Levi followed him. He stared at the bed. He felt hollow inside, but there was also a horrible mass of emotion hiding inside him, wanting to get loose and devour him.

She looked so small and pale. She had blood in her curls, and lots of wires crisscrossed from her skin to a machine beeping steadily beside her bed.

"I should never have touched her. I'm fucking cursed."

"This isn't your fault," Levi said.

"I was supposed to keep her safe. God, I'm crazy in love with her. Every bit of her. From the wild curls and sharp mind, to her fucking pretty toes. I love every inch of her." Ash reached out and gripped her hand. It was limp, but warm.

"I'll give you some time." Emerson swallowed, her eyes haunted. "We'll need to decide when to turn the machine off." The doctor's shoes were soundless as she walked away.

Ash made a pained, animal sound. The thought of turning off the machine keeping Marin's chest rising and falling almost killed Ash. Every muscle in his body was tense, and a part of him wanted to scream.

He'd just found her. This wasn't fucking fair.

But he knew better than most that life was never fair. No one promised you fair.

He heard a small gasp and looked up. A pale-skinned woman stood in the doorway. Selena was an alien woman, an enemy of the Gizzida who'd been abducted by them. Hell Squad had rescued her, and she'd found sanctuary at the Enclave. Her silver-white hair was loose around her shoulders, and she was holding a basket of fruit.

"Selena." Tane was watching her intently. "What are you doing in here?"

She looked up and stared at the squad leader. "I bring fresh fruit and flowers from the Garden for the patients." Her gaze went back to Marin. "Is she okay?"

Ash swallowed the lump in his throat. "No. No, she's not."

Selena moved over to Marin's bed. "I'm sorry she was hurt. She spent some time with me showing me a game on the comp."

Ash felt a spear of pain. "Pre-Emptive Strike."

Selena nodded. "I was terrible at it, but she never gave up."

"She can be pretty stubborn when it suits her." His voice broke.

"You love her?" Selena tilted her head, studying him.

"Yeah. Completely."

"We don't have a concept of romantic love on my planet. To us, everything is connected and intertwined.

To have only two people belong to each other is a foreign concept." She reached out and placed her hand on Marin's chest. "I see what love does to you, and I'm not sure if it is such a good thing."

"It's the best thing in the world, Selena," Ash said quietly. "Even when it hurts." He stroked Marin's hand. "Even knowing I'm going to lose her, I'd do it all again for the chance to love her, even just for a few days."

All of a sudden, he felt Marin's fingers flex on his. He frowned. Her skin was getting warmer.

He looked up and saw the alien woman's skin was glowing. "Selena?"

A rush of energy filled the room, lifting the hairs on Ash's arms.

"Selena." Tane's deep voice. He moved up behind the alien woman.

"I want to..." Selena's bright green eyes flashed.

Marin jerked up, gasping. Her eyes flew open, and the machine beside her started beeping madly.

Selena released Marin and stumbled backward. As she collapsed, Tane caught her before she hit the floor. Her green eyes fluttered closed, and her face was impossibly pale and drawn, her skin pulled tight over her cheekbones. Tane scooped her up into his arms.

"Selena," he growled.

Emerson slammed in. "What the hell is going on?" Her gaze landed on her patient. "Marin?"

Marin frowned. "Where am I? What happened?" She gripped Ash's hand. "We were fighting the raptors and trying to contain the virus—"

Ash just stared at her. Her face was glowing pink, her eyes alert.

His chest swelled. Unable to form any words, he climbed into the bed and pulled her into his arms.

She gripped him. "Ash?"

His hands tugged at the surgical gown she was wearing, tearing it open.

"Hey." She slapped at his hand, frowning.

Her wound was fully healed. There was just a faint pink scar beneath her breasts.

Emerson leaned over. "Oh, my God." She swiveled her head to look at Selena.

"Selena healed her," Ash said.

The alien woman was passed out, her body limp in Tane's arms.

"Doc?" Tane said.

Emerson hurried over, pressing a hand to Selena's neck. "Pulse is strong. She's fine. It looks like she expended a lot of energy to help Marin."

"What the hell did she just do?" Tane asked.

"I have no idea," Emerson replied. "She needs some rest. Let's find her a bed, and I'll give her a thorough check-up."

Tane frowned and pulled the woman's body closer. He followed the doc.

Ash pressed his face against Marin's curls, his chest tight. He could feel the steady beat of her heart against his chest. *Alive.* He still couldn't believe it.

He looked up and caught Levi's gaze. His best friend lifted his chin at Ash and then slipped out of the room.

Ash pulled back to look at Marin's face. "You're really okay?"

"I am. I think I could run a marathon," Marin said. "Maybe even take on a few more raptors."

He smiled at her. "I just saw that twitch beside your mouth."

She smiled back tiredly, snuggling into him. "Actually, I feel exhausted. I wouldn't mind a nap."

"I love you, Marin."

Her eyes went wide. "Really?"

"Really." His body was shaking and he pulled her closer. "All of you, Marin. Your sexy body, your cute face, your brilliant brain. I love that crease you get on your brow when you're working. The way you blink when you take off your glasses. Your sweet grin. I know you're too good for me, but I'm never letting you go."

Marin scrambled up onto her knees. "Do *not* put yourself down. Of course, you deserve me. You're brave and loyal and handsome."

He smiled at her. "Yes, ma'am. Anything else you want to tell me?"

She nodded and cupped his cheeks. "I love you, Ash Connors."

Oh, yeah. This hit of sweet felt really good. Then he saw her eyes were drooping.

"Tired," she murmured. "Will you hold me, Super-Soldier?"

Ash pulled her tighter against his chest. "Just try and get me to let you go."

Levi

SHIT. Levi strode down the corridor leading away from the infirmary. Seeing his friend so torn up had left him feeling shaken. He was glad as hell that Marin was going to be okay.

That meant Ash was going to be okay, too.

There was no better man than Ash Connors. The guy deserved love, a pretty woman, a sweet, easy life. He deserved it all.

God, it was something else to see his best buddy in love with a woman. Levi wouldn't have picked Marin for Ash, but he'd have been wrong. She really suited him. Opened up things in Ash that he'd ignored or kept choked off for a long time.

Levi stopped and leaned against the wall. Thankfully, the corridor was empty.

Levi had been married once. He'd made the tragic error of mistaking hot sex with a gorgeous biker babe for... more. Tiffany had been fun, and they'd burned up the sheets. Things had been sweet for a while.

Then things had gotten tough at the Iron Kings, and Levi had needed to focus on pulling the club over from the wrong fucking side of the law.

She'd resented the time he'd devoted to his club, had been jealous of Ash and his other brothers. She'd started plowing through his money, partying all the damn time, and then she'd started snorting shit up her nose.

God, the bitch had gotten nasty after that, and the fact that Levi had a temper and not a whole lot of patience for bullshit hadn't helped. He'd put up with her far longer than he should have...until all her scratching and snarling had made him hate her.

With a shake of his head, he headed down the tunnel. It had been a full-on day, and he didn't need to add the shit from the past to it. He needed a drink and something to take his mind off things.

He rounded the corner and slammed into someone heading the opposite direction.

Someone with auburn-red hair.

Chrissy stepped back and rolled her eyes. "You're like a bad smell."

"Not in the mood, Spitfire."

Her gaze skated over him, taking in his blood-stained, gore-splattered fatigues. Her face changed. "You were fighting the raptors. Are you okay?"

"I'm alive. Nothing a drink and a blow job won't fix."

Her mouth turned pinched. "You're such an asshole."

God, that sassy mouth of hers tempted him. His gaze dropped to her full lips. She had some sort of gloss on them, a faint pink color. All too easily, he could picture that mouth on his cock, her pretty lips stretched wide. She wouldn't get on her knees. She'd be above him, swallowing him deep, and letting him taste that pretty, little—

"Hey." She snapped her fingers in front of his face. "You in there, biker man?"

He blinked. "Yeah."

"You might want to shower before you proposition a woman to suck your cock. You really don't smell so good."

He arched a brow, his gut going tight. "You volunteering?"

She made a big show of looking both directions up and down the corridor.

"What are you looking for?" he asked.

"Nope. No flying pigs today." She smiled sweetly. "Guess you're out of luck. Sorry."

"I see the way you look at me, Spitfire." He stepped closer, expecting her to step back.

But Chrissy didn't back up. She held her ground until they were pressed together.

"I look at lots of things that I know aren't good for me," she said. "But I have this funny thing called *self-control*."

He touched a strand of her auburn hair. It was soft and shiny. "I'll give you a ride you won't forget."

"God, you are a grade-A asshole. Sorry, I like a little civilized wooing before I drop my panties."

The thought of her shimmying her panties down her long legs had his cock surging against his trousers. He leaned down. "I bet I could have you begging for my cock in just a few minutes."

Something flashed through her eyes. Then she shocked him by reaching out and grabbing his cock through his trousers.

Shit. Levi swallowed a groan. Instantly, he hardened.

She fondled him, then tilted her head. "Nope. I don't think this is worth begging for." She released him and stepped back. "Besides, I've had a better offer."

Levi narrowed his gaze. He rarely chased a woman. He had no need to. But something about this one set him aflame.

Suddenly, a small voice spoke from behind him. "Hey, Chrissy. You ready?"

Levi looked over his shoulder and saw a young boy watching them, curiosity in his eyes.

"Hey, Max." Chrissy hurried over to the boy and leaned down to give him a hug. "You okay after the attack?"

He nodded. "It was scary. Ruby, my foster sister, cried, but I didn't. I was brave and gave her a cuddle."

Chrissy stood, sliding an arm around him. "I'm proud of you. It's normal to be afraid, but to help someone else, that's being a true hero." Her gaze met Levi's over the boy's head.

Max looked at Levi, his gaze dropping to Levi's tattoos. "You're a berserker."

"Yeah." Levi lifted his chin.

"I saw the berserkers fighting when Chrissy and me were rescued from the aliens."

Chrissy shifted. "Max, remember that it's—"

"Chrissy and *I*," the boy said with exaggerated patience. He looked up at the woman. "She kept me safe, and I kept her safe."

She squeezed the boy. "We sure did."

"The berserkers are heroes, too."

A poorly-hidden grimace crossed Chrissy's face. "All the squads are heroes. Come on, let's go get that ice cream I promised you."

She turned the boy and they headed down the corridor. She didn't look back at Levi.

Levi blew out a breath. He really needed that drink.

As for the blow job...it appeared that there was only one set of lips that he wanted, now.

And one specific shade of hair that he wanted spread out on his pillow.

MARIN WORKED HER WIRELESS CONTROLLER, tapping the buttons. "These monsters are going down!" Then she frowned. "Ash, your character is walking into a wall." She looked over her shoulder.

She was sitting in the center of his bed, while he was sitting up against the headboard. His gaze was currently on her ass.

Marin was only wearing his Harley Davidson T-shirt and nothing else. In her excitement, she'd been bouncing up and down. "Ash?"

"Enjoying the view, Princess."

"You're going to wreck our high score." She dropped her controller and crawled toward him.

"I don't give a fuck."

She didn't either. She got close to him, breathing in his sexy, dark scent.

He dragged her into his lap and kissed her. Marin slid her tongue in to tangle with his, moaning into his mouth. She shifted closer, straddling one of his hard thighs. Oh, that felt so good. She rubbed against him, sensations rocketing through her.

Ash pulled his mouth from hers. "Hell, you fry my

brain. Unfortunately, we don't have time for this right now."

She ground against his leg again. "Yes, we do."

He groaned. "No, we have somewhere we need to be."

She frowned at him. She'd spent the last few days recovering from her injury, although she'd felt fine. Ash had confined her to his bed, mostly naked. That had translated into a lot of lazing around, playing Pre-Emptive Strike, having Ash bring her food, and having his clever mouth all over her. "Where?"

"It's a surprise." He patted her ass. "Get dressed and you'll see."

Marin pulled on her clothes, and took a second to try and tame her mass of curls.

"Leave 'em, Princess," he called out. "I like them wild."

Since Ash had shown her, in about a hundred different ways, how much he liked her curls, she dropped her hands and smiled. He especially liked tangling his hand in them when he was watching her suck his cock. A shiver of desire moved through her.

"Do we really have to go out?" she called out to him.

"Yes." He appeared out of the bathroom, wearing a clean set of jeans, and a crisp, white dress shirt.

She blinked at him. That shirt looked so good on him. Instantly, she imagined peeling it off.

"Marin, quit looking at me like that." He gripped her hips and steered her toward the door. "Out of here. Now. Had no idea when I fell for a cute, sexy geek, that she'd be wild in bed and insatiable."

Marin Mitchell was wild in bed. She grinned. He held her hand as they walked, and she soon realized they were heading toward the tech lab. Her pulse leaped. She hadn't been allowed back to work yet, and she had to admit, she was feeling a bit twitchy. She was ready to get back to it.

"I talked with Doc Emerson," Ash said.

Marin looked up at him. "Oh?"

"She's going to give me some advanced courses. I already had medic training that I kept up at the Iron Kings, but she's keen to put some courses together, for the future, for any kids who want to study medicine. She needs to pass the knowledge on."

Warmth burst inside Marin. "You're going to be her guinea pig."

He nodded. "I'm not leaving the squad. I like the squad and do good work there, too. But in my free time, I'll work with the doc."

"Doctor Ash Connors." Marin winked at him. "I can help. You can practice on me, and we can play doctor and patient."

He laughed, swatting her butt.

They reached the tech lab, and Ash pushed open the door and ushered her inside. They were met with a crowd of people.

"Surprise!"

Marin stared at everyone. She saw the tech team, Hell squad, Squad Nine, and the berserkers.

"What's this?" she asked. The tech benches, usually covered in tools and electronics, were loaded with food.

Shaw sauntered forward and put a homemade party hat on her head. "This is a 'Thanks for saving us' party."

From beside the sniper, Claudia winked. "Nice work, Curls."

At the back of the room, an entire bank of comp screens had been set up.

Levi cracked his knuckles. "We're having a Pre-Emptive Strike party. Geeks versus squads."

"Prepare to lose, soldier boy," Eric called out.

Levi spun and eyed the man.

Eric shrank back, holding his hands up. "Or not. Whatever works for you."

Laughter broke out around them. When Ash went to pour Marin a drink, Noah appeared. He was scowling.

"I need you back at work," he said. "If you can escape from your berserker. We still can't decrypt everything we managed to get from the data hub before we had to shut down the connection. Holmes had Elle holed up translating what we have so far, until Marcus threatened bodily harm and dragged her off."

"I'm ready to get back to work." Marin sighed. "I'm bummed that the aliens hacked us back and we couldn't keep the link open."

"We got data. It'll help. And none of us guessed the Gizzida would try what they did."

"How much damage did we sustain?" Ash had refused to discuss it with her.

"Lost some stores. It'll hurt, but we can still eat, and the doc is working to replicate more meds. We lost some spare parts and artwork."

Marin felt a hit of regret.

Noah gripped her shoulder. "The data will more than make up for it once we piece it all together. The main thing is, Holmes and Niko have been working around the clock. We've shored up the Enclave security to ensure the Gizzida can't get back in that way again. They cemented up the northern exit and closed down some damaged tunnels."

She nodded. "The virus?"

"Still have it contained." Noah gave her a smile. "Been waiting for my best tech to get her lazy butt out of bed and get to work studying it."

"Best tech, huh? Don't let Eric hear you say that."

"I expect to see you at your desk tomorrow." Noah nodded at her and slipped away.

Ash returned and handed her a drink. She sipped the champagne and scanned the room, watching as squad soldiers and tech team members sat down at the computers and started to play.

The world they'd once known was gone, but this was their world now. Where there were no barriers, no judgment, no prejudice. There were just survivors. People bonded together to survive. Doing their best to live their lives and thrive.

She leaned into Ash.

And in this world, a smart geek girl got to love a sexy biker bad boy.

Right here was a man who loved her inside and out. Her own personal, tattooed, sexy-as-hell super soldier.

"You want to play?" He nodded at the screen with a grin. "Whoever wins—" he leaned down and whispered in her ear. Hot, sexy promises.

Marin felt heat in her cheeks. "You're on, SuperSoldier. Prepare to go down."

He winked. "It'll be my pleasure, Princess."

I hope you enjoyed Ash and Marin's story!

Hell Squad continues with LEVI, starring another bad boy berserker of Squad Three. Coming in early 2018.

For more action-packed romance, read on for a preview of the first chapter of *Gladiator,* the first book in my best-winning Galactic Gladiators series.

Don't miss out! For updates about new releases, action romance info, free books, and other fun stuff, sign up for my VIP mailing list and get your *free box set* containing three action-packed romances.

Click here to get started: www.annahackettbooks.com

FREE BOX SET DOWNLOAD

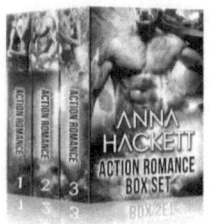

JOIN THE ACTION-PACKED ADVENTURE!

PREVIEW: GLADIATOR

MORE SCI-FI ROMANCE

Fighting for love, honor, and freedom on the galaxy's lawless outer rim.

Fighting for love, honor, and freedom on the galaxy's lawless outer rim...

When Earth space marine Harper Adams finds herself abducted by alien slavers off a space station, her life turns into a battle for survival. Dumped into an arena on a desert planet on the outer rim, she finds herself face to face with a big, tattooed alien gladiator...the champion of the Kor Magna Arena.

A former prince abandoned to the arena as a teen, Raiden Tiago has long ago earned his freedom. Now he rules the arena, but he doesn't fight for the glory, but instead for his own dark purpose—revenge against the Thraxian aliens who destroyed his planet. Then his existence is rocked by one small, fierce female fighter from an unknown planet called Earth.

Harper is determined to find a way home, but when she spots her best friend in the arena—a slave of the evil Thraxian aliens—she'll do anything to save her friend... even join forces with the tough, alpha male who sets her body on fire. But as Harper and Raiden step foot onto the blood-soaked sands of the arena, Harper worries that Raiden has his own dangerous agenda...

Just another day at the office.

Harper Adams pulled herself along the outside of the space station module. She could hear her quiet breathing inside her spacesuit, and she easily pulled her weightless body along the slick, white surface of the module. She stopped to check a security panel, ensuring all the systems were running smoothly.

Check. Same as it had been yesterday, and the day before that. But Harper never ever let herself forget that they were six hundred million kilometers away from Earth. That meant they were dependent only on themselves. She tapped some buttons on the security panel before closing the reinforced plastic cover. She liked to dot all her *I*s and cross all her *T*s. She never left anything to chance.

She grabbed the handholds and started pulling herself up over the cylindrical pod to check the panels on the other side. Glancing back behind herself, she caught a beautiful view of the planet below.

Harper stopped and made herself take it all in. The orange, white, and cream bands of Jupiter could take your breath away. Today, she could even see the famous super-storm of the Great Red Spot. She'd been on the Fortuna Research Station for almost eighteen months. That meant, despite the amazing view, she really didn't see it anymore.

She turned her head and looked down the length of the space station. At the end was the giant circular donut that housed the main living quarters and offices. The main ring rotated to provide artificial gravity for the residents. Lying off the center of the ring was the long cylinder of the research facility, and off that cylinder were several modules that housed various scientific labs and storage. At the far end of the station was the docking area for the supply ships that came from Earth every few months.

"Lieutenant Adams? Have you finished those checks?"

Harper heard the calm voice of her fellow space marine and boss, Captain Samantha Santos, through the comm system in her helmet.

"Almost done," Harper answered.

"Take a good look at the botany module. The computer's showing some strange energy spikes, but the scientists in there said everything looks fine. Must be a system malfunction."

Which meant the geek squad engineers were going to have to come in and do some maintenance. "On it."

Harper swung her body around, and went feet-first down the other side of the module. She knew the rest of the security team—all made up of United Nations Space Marines—would be running similar checks on the other modules across the station. They had a great team to ensure the safety of the hundreds of scientists aboard the station. There was also a dedicated team of engineers that kept the guts of the station running.

She passed a large, solid window into the module, and could see various scientists floating around benches filled with all kinds of plants. They all wore matching gray jumpsuits accented with bright-blue at the collars, that indicated science team. There was a vast mix of scientists and disciplines aboard—biologists, botanists, chemists, astronomers, physicists, medical experts, and the list went on. All of them were conducting experiments, and some were searching for alien life beyond the edge of the solar system. It seemed like every other week, more probes were being sent out to hunt for radio signals or collect samples.

Since humans had perfected large solar sails as a way to safely and quickly propel spacecraft, getting around the solar system had become a lot easier. With radiation pressure exerted by sunlight onto the mirrored sails, they could travel from Earth to Fortuna Station orbiting Jupiter in just a few months. And many of the scientists aboard the station were looking beyond the solar system, planning manned expeditions farther and farther away. Harper wasn't sure they were quite ready for that.

She quickly checked the adjacent control panel. Among all the green lights, she spotted one that was blinking red, and she frowned. They definitely had a problem with the locking system on the exterior door at the end of the module. She activated the small propulsion pack on her spacesuit, and circled around the module. She slowed down as she passed the large, round exterior door at the end of the cylindrical module.

It was all locked into place and looked secure.

As she moved back to the module, she grabbed a handhold and then tapped the small tablet attached to the forearm of her suit. She keyed in a request for maintenance to come and check it.

She looked up and realized she was right near another window. Through the reinforced glass, a pretty, curvy blonde woman looked up and spotted Harper. She smiled and waved. Harper couldn't help but smile and lifted her gloved hand in greeting.

Dr. Regan Forrest was a botanist and a few years younger than Harper. The young woman was so open and friendly, and had befriended Harper from her first day on the station. Harper had never had a lot of friends —mainly because she'd been too busy raising her younger sister and working. She'd never had time for girly nights out or gossip.

But Regan was friendly, smart, and had the heart of a steamroller under her pretty exterior. Harper always had trouble saying no to her. Maybe the woman reminded her a little of Brianna. At the thought of her sister, something twisted painfully in Harper's chest.

Regan floated over to the window and held up a small tablet. She'd typed in some words.

Cards tonight?

Harper had been teaching Regan how to play poker. The woman was terrible at it, and Harper beat her all the time. But Regan never gave up.

Harper nodded and held up two fingers to indicate a couple of hours. She was off-shift shortly, and then she had a sparring match with Regan's cousin, Rory—one of the station engineers—in the gym. Aurora "Call me Rory or I'll hit you" Fraser had been trained in mixed martial arts, and Harper found the female engineer a hell of a sparring partner. Rory was teaching Harper some martial arts moves and Harper was showing the woman some basic sword moves. Since she was little, Harper had been a keen fencer.

Regan grinned back and nodded. Then the woman's wide smile disappeared. She spun around, and through the glass Harper could see the other scientists all looking around, concerned. One scientist was spinning around, green plants floating in the air around him, along with fat droplets of water and some other green fluid. He'd clearly screwed up and let his experiment get free.

"Lieutenant Adams?" The captain's voice came through her helmet again. "Harper?"

There was a sense of urgency that made Harper's belly tighten. "Go ahead, Captain."

"We have an alarm sounding in the botany module. The computer says there is a risk of decompression."

Dammit. "I just checked the security panels. The

locking mechanism on the exterior door is showing red. I did a visual inspection and it's closed up tight."

"Okay, we talked with the scientist in charge. Looks like one of her team let something loose in there. It isn't dangerous, but it must be messing with the alarm sensors. System's locked them all in there." She made an annoyed sound. "Idiots will have to stay there until engineering can get down there and free them."

Harper studied the room through the glass again. Some of the green liquid had floated over to another bench that contained various frothing cylinders on it. A second later, the cylinders shattered, their contents bubbling upward.

The scientists all moved to the back exit of the module, banging on the locked door. *Damn.* They were trapped.

Harper met Regan's gaze. Her friend's face was pale, and wisps of her blonde hair had escaped her ponytail, floating around her face.

"Captain," Harper said. "Something's wrong. The experiments have overflowed their containment." She could see the scientists were all coughing.

"Engineering is on the way," the captain said.

Harper pushed herself off, flying over the surface of the module. She reached the control panel and saw that several other lights had turned red. They needed to get this under control and they needed to do it now.

"Harper!" The captain's panicked voice. "Decompression in progress!"

What the hell? The module jerked beneath Harper.

She looked up and saw the exterior door blow off, flying away from the station.

Her heart stopped. That meant all the scientists were exposed to the vacuum of space.

Fuck. Harper pushed off again, sending herself flying toward the end of the module. She put her arms by her sides to help increase her speed. Through the window, she saw that most of the scientists had grabbed on to whatever they could hold on to. A few were pulling emergency breathers over their heads.

She reached the end of the pod and saw the damage. There was torn metal where the door had been ripped off. Inside the door, she knew there would be a temporary repair kit containing a sheet of high-tech nano fabric that could be stretched across the opening to reestablish pressure. But it needed to be put in place manually. Harper reached for the latch to release the repair kit.

Suddenly, a slim body shot out of the pod, her arms and legs kicking. Her mouth was wide open in a silent scream.

Regan. Harper didn't let herself think. She turned, pushed off and fired her propulsion system, arrowing after her friend.

"Security Team to the botany module," she yelled through her comm system. "Security Team to botany module. We have decompression. One scientist has been expelled. I'm going after her. I need someone that can help calm the others and get the module sealed again."

"Acknowledged, Lieutenant," Captain Santos answered. "I'm on my way."

Harper focused on reaching Regan. She was gaining

on her. She saw that the woman had lost consciousness. She also knew that Regan had only a couple of minutes to survive out here. Harper let her training take over. She tapped the propulsion system controls, trying for more speed, as she maneuvered her way toward Regan.

As she got close, Harper reached out and wrapped her arm around the scientist. "I've got you."

Harper turned, at the same time clipping a safety line to the loops on Regan's jumpsuit. Then, she touched the controls and propelled them straight back towards the module. She kept her friend pulled tightly toward her chest. *Hold on, Regan.*

She was so still. It reminded Harper of holding Brianna's dead body in her arms. Harper's jaw tightened. She wouldn't let Regan die out here. The woman had dreamed of working in space, and worked her entire career to get here, even defying her family. Harper wasn't going to fail her.

As the module got closer, she saw that the security team had arrived. She saw the captain's long, muscled body as she and another man put up the nano fabric.

"Incoming. Keep the door open."

"Can't keep it open much longer, Adams," the captain replied. "Make it snappy."

Harper adjusted her course, and, a second later, she shot through the door with Regan in her arms. Behind her, the captain and another huge security marine, Lieutenant Blaine Strong, pulled the stretchy fabric across the opening.

"Decompression contained," the computer intoned.

Harper released a breath. On the panel beside the

door, she saw the lights turning green. The nano fabric wouldn't hold forever, but it would do until they got everyone out of here, and then got a maintenance team in here to fix the door.

"Oxygen levels at required levels," the computer said again.

"Good work, Lieutenant." Captain Sam Santos floated over. She was a tall woman with a strong face and brown hair she kept pulled back in a tight ponytail. She had curves she kept ruthlessly toned, and golden skin she always said was thanks to her Puerto Rican heritage.

"Thanks, Captain." Harper ripped her helmet off and looked down at Regan.

Her blonde hair was a wild tangle, her face was pale and marked by what everyone who worked in space called space hickeys—bruises caused by the skin's small blood vessels bursting when exposed to the vacuum of space. *Please be okay*.

"Here." Blaine appeared, holding a portable breather. The big man was an excellent marine. He was about six foot five with broad shoulders that stretched his spacesuit to the limit. She knew he was a few inches over the height limit for space operations, but he was a damn good marine, which must have gone in his favor. He had dark skin thanks to his African-American father and his handsome face made him popular with the station's single ladies, but mostly he worked and hung out with the other marines.

"Thanks." Harper slipped the clear mask over Regan's mouth.

"Nice work out there." Blaine patted her shoulder. "She's alive because of you."

Suddenly, Regan jerked, pulling in a hard breath.

"You're okay." Harper gripped Regan's shoulder. "Take it easy."

Regan looked around the module, dazed and panicky. Harper watched as Regan caught sight of the fabric stretched across the end of the module, and all the plants floating around inside.

"God," Regan said with a raspy gasp, her breath fogging up the dome of the breather. She shook her head, her gaze moving to Harper. "Thanks, Harper."

"Any time." Harper squeezed her friend's shoulder. "It's what I'm here for."

Regan managed a wan smile. "No, it's just you. You didn't have to fly out into space to rescue me. I'm grateful."

"Come on. We need to get you to the infirmary so they can check you out. Maybe put some cream on your hickeys."

"Hickeys?" Regan touched her face and groaned. "Oh, no. I'm going to get a ribbing."

"And you didn't even get them the pleasurable way."

A faint blush touched Regan's cheeks. "That's right. If I had, at least the ribbing would have been worth it."

With a relieved laugh, Harper looked over at her captain. "I'm going to get Regan to the infirmary."

The other woman nodded. "Good. We'll meet you back at the Security Center."

With a nod, Harper pushed off, keeping one arm around Regan, and they floated into the main part of the science facility. Soon, they moved through the entrance into the central hub of the space station. As the artificial gravity hit, Harper's boots thudded onto the floor. Beside her, Regan almost collapsed.

Harper took most of the woman's weight and helped her down the corridor. They pushed into the infirmary.

A gray-haired, barrel-chested man rushed over. "Decided to take an unscheduled spacewalk, Dr. Forrest?"

Regan smiled weakly. "Yes. Without a spacesuit."

The doctor made a tsking sound and then took her from Harper. "We'll get her all patched up."

Harper nodded. "I'll come and check on you later."

Regan grabbed her hand. "We have a blackjack game scheduled. I'm planning to win back all those chocolates you won off me."

Harper snorted. "You can try." It was good to see some life back in Regan's blue eyes.

As Harper strode out into the corridor, she ran a hand through her dark hair, tension slowly melting out of her shoulders. She really needed a beer. She tilted her neck one way and then the other, hearing the bones pop.

Just another day at the office. The image of Regan drifting away from the space station burst in her head. Harper released a breath. She was okay. Regan was safe and alive. That was all that mattered.

With a shake of her head, Harper headed toward the Security Center. She needed to debrief with the captain and clock off. Then she could get out of her spacesuit and take the one-minute shower that they were all allotted.

That was the one thing she missed about Earth. Long,

hot showers.

And swimming. She'd been a swimmer all her life and there were days she missed slicing through the water.

She walked along a long corridor, meeting a few people—mainly scientists. She reached a spot where there was a long bank of windows that afforded a lovely view of Jupiter, and space beyond it.

Stingy showers and unscheduled spacewalks aside, Harper had zero regrets about coming out into space. There'd been nothing left for her on Earth, and to her surprise, she'd made friends here on Fortuna.

As she stared out into the black, mesmerized by the twinkle of stars, she caught a small flash of light in the distance. She paused, frowning. What the hell was that?

She stared hard at the spot where she'd seen the flash. Nothing there but the pretty sprinkle of stars. Harper shook her head. Fatigue was playing tricks on her. It had to have just been a weird trick of the lights reflecting off the glass.

Pushing the strange sighting away, she continued on to the Security Center.

Galactic Gladiators
Gladiator
Warrior
Hero
Protector
Champion
Barbarian
Also Available as Audiobooks!

PREVIEW: AMONG GALACTIC RUINS

MORE ACTION ROMANCE?

ACTION
ADVENTURE
TREASURE HUNTS
SEXY SCI-FI ROMANCE

When astro-archeologist and museum curator Dr. Lexa Carter discovers a secret map to a lost old Earth treasure—a priceless Fabergé egg—she's excited at the prospect of a treasure hunt to the dangerous desert planet of Zerzura. What she's not so happy about is being saddled with a bodyguard—the museum's mysterious new head of security, Damon Malik.

After many dangerous years as a galactic spy, Damon

Malik just wanted a quiet job where no one tried to kill him. Instead of easy work in a museum full of artifacts, he finds himself on a backwater planet babysitting the most infuriating woman he's ever met.

She thinks he's arrogant. He thinks she's a trouble-magnet. But among the desert sands and ruins, adventure led by a young, brash treasure hunter named Dathan Phoenix, takes a deadly turn. As it becomes clear that someone doesn't want them to find the treasure, Lexa and Damon will have to trust each other just to survive.

The Phoenix Adventures

Among Galactic Ruins
At Star's End
In the Devil's Nebula
On a Rogue Planet
Beneath a Trojan Moon
Beyond Galaxy's Edge
On a Cyborg Planet
Return to Dark Earth
On a Barbarian World
Lost in Barbarian Space
Through Uncharted Space

Reed

Roth

Noah

Shaw

Holmes

Niko

Finn

Theron

Hemi

Ash

Also Available as Audiobooks!

The Anomaly Series

Time Thief

Mind Raider

Soul Stealer

Salvation

Anomaly Series Box Set

The Phoenix Adventures

Among Galactic Ruins

At Star's End

In the Devil's Nebula

On a Rogue Planet

Beneath a Trojan Moon

Beyond Galaxy's Edge

On a Cyborg Planet

Return to Dark Earth

On a Barbarian World

Lost in Barbarian Space

Through Uncharted Space

Perma Series

Winter Fusion

A Galactic Holiday

Warriors of the Wind

Tempest

Storm & Seduction

Fury & Darkness

Standalone Titles

Savage Dragon

Hunter's Surrender

One Night with the Wolf

For more information visit AnnaHackettBooks.com

ABOUT THE AUTHOR

I'm a USA Today bestselling author and I'm passionate about **_action romance_**. I love stories that combine the thrill of falling in love with the excitement of action, danger and adventure. I'm a sucker for that moment when the team is walking in slow motion, shoulder-to-shoulder heading off into battle. I write about people overcoming unbeatable odds and achieving seemingly impossible goals. I like to believe it's possible for all of us to do the same.

My books are mixture of action, adventure and sexy romance and they're recommended for anyone who enjoys fast-paced stories where the boy wins the girl at the end (or sometimes the girl wins the boy!)

For release dates, action romance info, free books, and other fun stuff, sign up for the latest news here:

Website: www.annahackettbooks.com